LONG *after*

FATHERS

To Mary Ellen,
I hope that these
stories sing to you.

LONG *after*

FATHERS

Roberta REES

COTEAU
BOOKS

Edited by Sandra Birdsell.
Cover and series design by Duncan Campbell.
Cover photo: "Woman's Hair Blowing in Wind" by Kamil Vojnar, Photonica collection/Getty Images.

Printed and bound in Canada at Marquis Bookprinting.
This book is printed on 100% recycled paper.

Library and Archives Canada Cataloguing in Publication

Rees, Roberta
Long after fathers / Roberta Rees.

ISBN 978-1-55050-358-6

1. Crowsnest Pass (Alta. and B.C.)—Fiction. I. Title.
PS8585.E434L65 2007   C813'.54   C2007-901736-3

10 9 8 7 6 5 4 3 2 1

2517 Victoria Ave.
Regina, Saskatchewan
Canada   S4P 0T2

AVAILABLE IN CANADA & THE US FROM
Fitzhenry & Whiteside
195 Allstate Parkway
Markham, ON, Canada, L3R 4T8

The publisher gratefully acknowledges the financial assistance of the Saskatchewan Arts Board, the Canada Council for the Arts, the Government of Canada through the Book Publishing Industry Development Program (BPIDP), Association for the Export of Canadian Books, and the City of Regina Arts Commission, for its publishing program.

Canada Council
for the Arts
Conseil des Arts
du Canada

ARTS BOARD

Canadä

I dedicate this book to:

my mother, Evelyn J. Rees
my siblings, Carol, Allen and David
my nieces, Mikaila, Alex, Megan, Rachael and Olivia
my nephew, Aidan
the memory of my father, Robert Rees

CONTENTS

JESSIE

Lucky Strike

SUPPER. THE LAST SUPPER, JESSIE THOUGHT, before her five brothers came home from the farms Daddy sent them to. "No choice," he'd said last spring, the last brother, nine years old, heading down the road on foot clutching his bag to his chest, away from their house between the railyards and spur lines and warehouses and factories.

Jessie had stayed out in the middle of the road, watched Jordie's shoes flap, his naked heels, until he became a stick wavering on the horizon ."He'll drink up your wages," she'd whispered to his stick back, "then he'll drink you up too."

Jessie looked around the table — five empty places like Mummy's missing teeth from the time Mummy stepped between Daddy and one of the kids. The last night to take him on, take him down, but he had to be drunk, drunker than now. And away from Mummy.

Jessie smiled at Daddy, eating dainty with his knife and fork at the head of the table.

She smiled at Gabrielle sitting between her and Daddy, but Gabrielle's eyes had that faraway look. Jessie smiled across the table at her oldest sister, Elona, her eyes behind her round wire-frame glasses flicking between Mummy at one end and Daddy at the other.

Jessie smiled at Mummy. Mummy looked at Daddy quietly cutting and chewing, eyes on his plate, her skinny face hungry with shadows, then let her brown-black eyes rest on Jessie's.

Through the shadows, through the dark circles around Mummy's eyes, Jessie felt the way she always did when Mummy smiled at her – hot and shivering. Her hand tingled to reach out and stroke Mummy's toothless bottom lip, soft and puckered, but not now, not with Daddy sitting here quiet, pretending he wasn't looking at them, pretending he wasn't hearing their chewing and swallowing and Mummy's breath getting wheezy. But he was watching and listening, all loose around the shoulders. Waiting.

Solemn as a prayer, Daddy poised his cutlery on the edge of his plate, pushed his plate back. Graceful as a high-wire dancer, he reached for his can of Lucky Strike tobacco, gentled it open, reached it out to Gabrielle beside him. "Take a whiff," he whispered.

Jessie looked from Daddy's soft-pursed mouth to his hands. Puff-knuckled and square. Boxer's hands.

"Come on, take a whiff." Daddy held the open can under Gabrielle's nose, his fingers gentle around the tin, his middle finger covering the word "Strike." Just "Lucky," plain old "Lucky."

Gabrielle stared at Daddy, her profile pointy and stubborn.

Jessie looked at Mummy at the other end of the table from Daddy, the long hungry shadows swallowing Mummy's eyes and cheeks. Mummy stared at Daddy's hand around the tin. "Lucky. Lucky."

Daddy shook his tin. "Don't look so serious, Gab. Costs nothing to smell."

Gabrielle narrowed her eyes.

"Come on, girl." Daddy's other hand flew from his side toward Gabrielle faster than she could flinch.

Mummy opened her mouth.

Daddy floated his hand down on top of Gabrielle's smooth hair. "A chip off the old block, hey Gab? Just like your old man." He stroked her head.

Gabrielle's face flushed almost as red as Daddy's. His fingers making curls in Gabrielle's hair, Daddy lifted his face to Mummy way at the other end of the table, smiled.

Gabrielle narrowed her eyes sideways at Daddy's turned-away face, pursed her lips. A foamy drool of spit rolled off her bottom lip, into Daddy's tin.

A bubble rose from Jessie's stomach, up into the back of her throat. She clamped her lips shut.

Across the table Elona stared at Daddy's finger blocking out the word "Strike," her eyes blank behind her round wire glasses. Mummy wheezed, coughed.

Jessie held the bubble in her throat with her tongue. Oh Daddy, Daddy, your nose looks like a strawberry.

Daddy's fingers slid off Gabrielle's smooth hair, dipped into his tin. He looked at Gabrielle, narrowed his eyes.

His fist flew.

Past Gabrielle.

Toward Jessie.

Now, Jessie thought, now, white blur flying for her face, his fist too fast, always too fast.

The heat of his knuckle on the tip of her nose, Daddy pulled his punch, laughed, his blue eyes pretend-pleading. "Take a deep sniff, Pug. Some poor bugger picked these leaves."

He looked down the table at Mummy, her head cocked to one side, her eyes lost in shadow. "Some poor bugger without any meat or vegetables, because he doesn't have a wife like your mother. Your mother's a fine woman. Keeps you clothed and fed and God, I love that woman."

The cords in Mummy's throat pushed up under her skin.

Jessie lifted one hand, clamped it over her mouth.

Daddy's head swiveled. He looked down at Jessie, at his hand holding tobacco under her nose. "You little swine." One eyebrow shot up. "I said take a whiff, you ungrateful little swine."

Jessie bit the palm of her hand. Not yet. Not now. Not here. "Fat ugly strawberry," she whispered into her hand.

Daddy scraped his chair back, lunged for her.

"Don't you touch her." Elona's voice, hard and flat, eyes sharp through her glasses, focused on Daddy.

"Bite," Jessie pushed her teeth into her hand, "bite."

Daddy's fingers brushed the tip of Jessie's nose, the back of her hand, her chin. He was on his feet, dancing on his toes, around behind her, around behind Mummy, waltzing up behind Elona, pinkie fingers in the air, lifting Elona's glasses off her face, laying them gently beside her plate. "What did you say?"

He dropped down on one knee, cupped Elona's face in his hands, slid a fingertip up her cheek, around her wide-open naked eyes, one eye turned in. "You could have been so beautiful." Daddy's finger stroked the skin over Elona's temple. "If only I could kiss your eye straight." He pulled her face toward him.

"Stop it." Mummy's voice echoed off the walls. Her eyes burned at Daddy from deep in their sockets.

Daddy looked up at her, his eyes half closed.

"I said stop it." Mummy pressed her arms to her sides, her lips tight.

His hands cupping Elona's face, Daddy stared up at Mummy, his piercing-through-you look. Red flushed up his cheeks.

So still. Holding their breath. Under the table, Jessie clenched her fists.

Still staring at Mummy, Daddy slid his hands off Elona's face.

The sound of their heartbeats.

Jessie slid to the edge of her seat.

Nothing moved, not even the skin around his eyes, but his whole look changed, went soft and sincere again at Mummy. "Celia, Celia, if only you were a tulip and I were a red red rose."

Still all soft, his hands hanging dead at his sides, he pulled himself up, stepped – feet wide, careful – over to Jessie. "Next time, Pug, block with both your fists."

Then he was gone, out the door.

"THIS CAME FROM. Before. Your Dad." Mummy panted, she and Jessie alone in Mummy and Daddy's bedroom, the door closed, the lamp beside the bed turned on. Through the door muffled bang of pots and Elona's singing, *There'll be bluebirds over, the white cliffs of Dover, tomorrow just you wait and see.*

Trembling, shoulders strained up to her ears, Mummy knelt beside the bed, lifted a dress, folded, arms pinned back, from her steamer trunk. The dress unfurled, puff of sweetpea and moth balls and dust, hid Mummy's face, her skinny arms and knees, hung black and shivery between them. Behind the dress Mummy coughed, a strangled cough.

Her bum on the edge of the bed, Jessie waited for Mummy to catch her breath, for Mummy to look over the dress at her.

Jessie craned her neck to look up at the picture of Jesus over the bed, his heart on the outside of his robe, his hands open to Jessie like he wanted to hug her. Cold, his hands were probably cold like Mummy's before her adrenaline shots when she panted and her heart beat so slow Jessie held her breath, her hand on Mummy's wrist, "Come on, come on."

6

If Jessie were alive back then, she would have held Jesus' hands between her own. She would have kissed them the way she did Mummy's, pressed her lips against his palms.

Mummy draped the dress over Jessie's knees, her eyes glassy and far away, her lips open, gasping for air. Her skinny arms and legs and neck poked out of her slip. *Robin Hood*, her slip said on the front, *Robin Hood Flour Mills Ltd*. Her whole body quaking, she rubbed her dress over Jessie's knees. "We used to. Dress up. Go dancing." She raised her eyes to Jessie, smiled. "Your dad. And me."

Jessie's eyes flicked from one of Mummy's eyes to the other, down Mummy's hollow cheeks to her open lips. She could put her lips on Mummy's, taste Mummy's heart beating slow and weak, take Mummy's panting breath and hold it deep inside until she could breathe out slow and long for her. Then Mummy could get up every morning, she could sing or dance or beat the rugs or walk beside the river, speak long sentences.

Mummy's eyes, dark rings around them. "He's a. Good man. Jess. When sober. Not the same. Person. Used to fish. No matter. How cold. Cooked trout. Under. The train bridge. Fed the men. Riding the rails. Joked he was. Jesus." Mummy slumped forward, reached around Jessie, gasped. "For you. My dress." Picked up the bottle of adrenaline and her needle. Handed them to Jessie. Fell onto her side.

Jessie held the tiny glass bottle up in front of her, dunked the tip of the needle into the bottle, pulled up on the plunger, turned the needle upside down, flicked with her middle finger.

She knelt beside Mummy, watched her own square fingers slide Mummy's slip up over Mummy's bones, rub the thin skin on Mummy's hip, sink the needle in, press the plunger.

One. Two. Three. She shuffled sideways on her knees so she could look in Mummy's face. Mummy's eyes opened wide. She coughed. Gagged. Jessie reached under the bed for the pot, held it for Mummy, turned her head away.

"I need to rest, Jess." Mummy's voice fast and shaking. Jessie set the pot on the bedside table, wrapped an arm lightly over Mummy's shoulder, pressed her hand against Mummy's sweaty back. Mummy's heart jumped, crashed against her ribs. Against Jessie's cupped palm.

Jessie looked up at Jesus with his heart on the outside, his palms out. Her own heart beat hard. She put her lips on Mummy's forehead, kissed a bead of sweat, cold and salty.

JESSIE CREPT THROUGH THE KITCHEN, Elona and Gabrielle side-by-side over the sink, shoulders touching, heads bent, made her feet carry her past them, her hand aching to reach up and touch the backs of their necks.

Upstairs, she tucked Mummy's dress under her pillow, tiptoed back down to the kitchen, knees weak.

"You okay, kiddo?" Elona turned from the sudsy pan, her face soft, her sleeves rolled up. The muscles in her forearms flexed. The war ended two years ago, but International Biscuit Company kept Elona on. Fast and runty as the rest of them, muscles round and hard, she could lift sacks of flour and sugar, run the heavy machines as well as the men. Muscled like Daddy, but without the fists.

"I'm good." Jessie put on her ball cap. "I'm going out for a walk. See you in an hour."

JESSIE WAITED OUTSIDE THE Inner City Boxing Club, her hair shoved up under one of her brother's caps. She slouched against the brick wall, turned her head away whenever the door opened and a boy stepped out, sweat matting his hair.

When the door stopped opening and closing, she straightened up, wiped her sweaty palms down her overalls, pulled her shoulders back, sauntered through the door, toward the ring, breathing deeply through her nose – muggy, sweaty air, old leather and aftershave.

Toward Laddy Jones, leaning his forearms on the ropes, eyes turned up to the empty ring. Jessie walked around the ring, stood beside him, leaned her arms on the ropes, turned her eyes up.

Laddy was quiet for a long time. Jessie's heart beat fast. A bead of sweat rolled down her back.

"Your old man just came by. Says you want to fight." Laddy's voice sounded far away.

Jessie held herself still, stared at the mat, the ropes.

"Said he'd wrap the ropes for free if I train you to box. I said 'what about those scrappy boys?' He said you're the one comes with him to the matches, you're the one wants to learn to fight. Said he's taught you some already."

Jessie's face burned; she could tell without looking up that he was looking down at the top of her head. "Well, let's throw some gloves on you, see what you can do."

Jessie stood in the middle of the ring, lifted her gloves in front of her face. She glared overtop her fists at Laddy, bounced on the balls of her feet. He stared back at her, arms down at his sides.

"Okay, kid, dance."

Jessie knew what he meant, but couldn't help it. She dropped her gloves, broke into a heel-shuffle-toe tap dance.

Laddy threw his head back, laughed out loud. "You're weird kid. A bit of your old man in you. Now really dance."

Jessie raised her fists, danced. Solid. Balanced. Toward Laddy, away. Left, right. She jabbed at his chest. Her glove connected.

Heat ran down her arm. She brought her glove back to cover her nose and cheek, feinted right, hit his shoulder with a left hook.

"Hold it, kid. Take it easy." But she was moving in, a solid right to his chin. He put his hand out to stop her. A stab of heat burst over her eye. Flamed straight to her gloves. Left. Right. Feint right. Fast. From the shoulder. Someone breathing hard. Someone saying "Stop," but she couldn't stop. The burning in her legs, her fists. Until he couldn't get up, could never raise his fists to Mummy again. He was moving toward her, arms out, eyes pleading. He was sober, smiling, he was the one taught her to hit a home run, throw a perfect pitch. Proud of her, he said, 'I'm so proud of you.' Raised a bottle to his lips. Raised his fists. Heat waves making her eyes burn, Jessie aimed for his nose. "You could kill a man that way," he said, "knock his nose up into his brain."

His arms grabbed her in a headlock, held her face to his chest. That man smell. Soap and talc and tobacco. "Take it easy, kid. It's okay. You're okay. That happens, you take a hit and you can't stop. Take a deep breath, kid."

Laddy Jones dropped his arms, looked into her eyes. "Jesus Christ, you have more speed and instinct than most of the boys who hang out here. As a professional trainer, all I can say is too bad you're a girl."

MUMMY'S WOOL DRESS kissing her skin, Jessie lay curled tight against Gabrielle's back, her forehead pressed to one of the gristly buds on Gabrielle's shoulder blades.

"You could have been an angel," Mummy told Gabrielle on the nights Mummy could breathe enough to climb up the stairs to their bedroom, "you could have been an angel, but you gave up your wings to live with us."

Before she left, Elona had pulled her Army Surplus wool trousers and sweater over her yellow flowered dress. "I'm off, Jess. Look in on Mom before you go to bed, kiddo, she's wheezing and coughing bad." She rested her hands on Jessie's shoulders. "She'll be okay, Jess." Elona licked her lips, dry from the wind and work, kissed Jessie on the forehead.

Jessie looked up into Elona's naked eyes, the turned in one making her look confused. Jessie couldn't tell if Elona was looking right at her or at something just behind her. Elona leaned over, put her hands on the sides of Jessie's face, her nose close to Jessie's. Both her eyes turned in then, looked right into Jessie's. "You're wound too tight, kiddo. Go to bed early."

Gabrielle fell asleep with a sigh. Jessie lay awake, muscles tense, ready.

Downstairs, the kitchen door opened, a breeze blew up the stairway. Jessie nudged Gabrielle's shoulder, "You awake?"

Gabrielle murmured in her sleep, "Mama?"

Jessie grit her teeth, listened for the thump of his boots, his slurred voice. Where the hell are you, woman? Come take my boots off.

Fast. She had to move fast, catch him before he yelled. She rolled off the bed, Mummy's dress shivering down her thighs, landed light on her feet, already moving across the room, fists up in front of her face.

Downstairs, the kitchen floor creaked. Soft footsteps crossed the kitchen linoleum, into the living room, toward Mummy and Daddy's bedroom.

Fast. She had to stop him before he crept in there, before he could raise his voice, his fists. The balls of her feet barely touched the stairs. Mummy's dress flicked her shins.

The footsteps stopped. A bitter taste burned the back of Jessie's throat.

"Hello?" Mummy called out into the darkness, her voice thick and weak.

Jessie's feet slid off the bottom step. She ran through the dark. Close, he was close to Mummy, she had to catch him.

"It's me, Mom, Elona."

Jessie dropped her fists, squeezed her eyes shut. Elona standing there in the dark doorway, listening to Mummy wheeze, the way Jessie was tonight, before she went upstairs.

If Jessie weren't crying, she would have tiptoed through the dark to Mummy's bedroom, held Elona's hand, kissed her knuckles dry and flaky from working at IBC Biscuits. Burying her nose in the collar of Mummy's dress, she turned toward the stairs, so far away in the dark.

Later, when he came in, she would move faster, catch him at the back door, the shiver and sweetpea of Mummy's dress bearing down on him before he could make out who was wearing it.

Shaking, she tiptoed upstairs, slid under the covers beside Gabrielle, lay on her back, counted Elona's footsteps creaking up the stairs, across the landing into their bedroom. Without a word, Elona brushed past Jessie and Gabrielle's bed, brushed the palm of her hand over Jessie's lips. Salt and butter and sugar.

On the other side of the room, Elona undressed in the dark. First, the click of her glasses on the dresser, the slide of her sweater and pants, the sigh of her dress off her shoulders, down her arms.

If the moon were up, by the light of the moon, the silvery moon, Jessie would see tiny yellow flowers slip down over Elona's breasts, her hips. She would see Elona bend over, roll a cotton stocking down her thigh, her muscles flexed.

If there were a moon, a silvery moon.

Iodine

ICOTINE-TEETH. JESSIE SAW THEM AS SOON as he stepped out from behind the pillar of Lowney's warehouse two doors down from her house. A perfect stranger – grey fedora, tweed jacket, lips pulling back a smile. "Pardon me for being so bold, little girl, but you are the spitting image of Shirley Temple."

Clean hat, clean jacket, hands in his pockets, blue cut-sky eyes, soft-as-clouds voice. But his teeth – streaked brown and yellow. "Of course, she's famous, that Shirley Temple. Now I'll bet you wouldn't mind being famous, would you?"

Two thudding heart beats Jessie stared into the sun and shadows flicking through the shards in the man's eyes. At the stained teeth falling for her eye. Her heart crashing into her ribs, she spun back toward her house, Mummy's name in her throat.

He spun her back fast, squeezed out Mummy's name broken and breathless, his hand hard over her mouth, his voice in her ear. "You know how Shirley Temple got famous, little girl?"

She twisted her head, exploded. Threw herself back.

His arms and hands tightened. "I can break your neck, kid, your mother's neck, or I can make you famous. You choose."

Past the red brick factories and warehouses and the Ashdowns' house and the Kiyookas' and Uncle Joe and Auntie Margaret's — two-storey wooden homes among the factories and warehouses.

Away from her home, bleached grey in the sun next to Dench's Truckyard. Away from Mummy propped up in bed clawing her chest for air.

"Shirley, Shirley, my curly girly Shirley." His voice knotted in her hair, his teeth brushed her scalp, all the way along 10th Avenue across from the train tracks. Her avenue, and not a neighbour, not one of her five brothers or two sisters or any of their friends or warehouse workers, not anyone she knew out hanging sheets or drinking canned heat or trading marbles, no one to release her from his arms crushing her, his hand choking her voice.

The stranger's breath burned the top of her head. "My daughter — she's been a bad girl and she needs discipline." He laughed, smiled at the men and women walking up and down the sidewalk as if it was theirs. As if it was his.

Her home. Her street. Her brothers and sisters and friends and the men in the train yards on the other side who gave her broken watermelon to take home and the men in the pits under the trucks who gave her bolts and pieces of metal and the women from the poultry place on the corner who gave her chicken fat and Pearl Harbour passed out on the train tracks until Jessie or one of her brothers or sisters hauled her off.

Jessie thrashed her head, growled. He cinched tighter, thumbed one of her nostrils shut.

No one she knew. No one knew her.

Strangers with hooded eyes in the sun watched him drag her. His hand stank like rotten fish and sick-sweet aftershave. His breath burned in her ear. "Famous. I can make you famous."

Out of town along the tracks along the Bow River eating green and gurgling into the riverbank, over crunching yellow leaves.

Away. Away from Mummy. I want my. I need my.

Her body. Her running, boxing, flying eleven-year-old body.

Her chest, her belly, her thighs.

His teeth.

Her blood.

His fists.

"A rock." His teeth falling in her face. "To finish you off. You'll be famous. I will have made you a star."

Her arms, her legs, her heart beating Mummy Mummy Mummy.

Lift her from the tall grass and dead leaves, drag her to the Bow River miles upstream from their house, the fast deep green river. I can't swim. I need my.

She doesn't remember crossing, river in her mouth and eyes, Mummy's name in her throat. His poison burning her raw inside.

She remembers running along Memorial Drive beside the river, screaming, knocking on doors. Blood ran down her legs, the old woman she didn't know in this strange part of the city opened her door, wrapped her in her arms, "Oh darling."

The policewoman, the only policewoman in the city, held her in a blanket in the back seat of the police car, "Let's get you to your mother, you need your mother."

PROPPED UP ON FOUR PILLOWS, Cecilia Denise clawed at her chest. Her bedroom, her bleached house, her eight hungry children, her bottle-ruined husband, the smell of horse blowing over from the race track down the road, pinned her to her bed, crushed the breath out of her.

On the wall above her Jesus held out his palms. "Come with me Cecilia Denise."

Her eyelids flickered. The house shifted, settled, snapped two of her ribs. A pain pierced her heart. "I can't. Who'll feed them? They're too young."

On the outside of his chest, Jesus' heart beat red, orange. "They're old enough. Your oldest girl will look after them."

Suffocating for air, her body arched into spasm. Sweat stung her eyes. "Please. If I could. Breathe."

But Jesus was gone and her own dead mother looked down at her, a light in her black eyes, her heart on the outside of her dress. "*Viens ici*, Cecile. I couldn't breathe either, now look at me."

Her mother held out her hand, brown and calloused, "*Viens ici*. A mother always loves her children."

That's when the policewoman brought her in, trembling, whimpering – Jessie, her special girl, her always-laughing, tap-dancing, home-run girl.

"Can't," Cecilia Denise moaned, adrenalin hitting her heart, pulling her up out of her sick bed. "Merde merde merde," she unwrapped the bloody blanket from her daughter, ran her fingertips over the punctures and bruises in her child's skin.

"Look at me." She held her daughter's face in the palms of her hands, stared into Jessie's green drowning eyes. "This was not your fault. You did nothing wrong. You remember that."

Hungry for her own mother, she pulled Jessie's head to her breast, cradled her child against her drowning heart. "You'll be okay, baby, you'll be okay."

NOT JESSIE'S FATHER, booze-roughened or toffee-sober.

Not her oldest brother, who used to do up her snowsuit and take her skating, that gone away look in his eyes.

Not her shoulder-swaying swaggering brother.

Not her beloved jigging-like-a-leprechaun brother, his eyes turned down at the outside corners so he always had a laugh-cry face.

Not her green-eyed golden-haired brother breaking their hearts.

Not even Jordie, her nine-year-old brother, born without a lining in his stomach, the sheep-lining in his stomach since he was three and came home from the hospital shock-eyed and stick-skinny and had to learn to walk and talk all over.

Only Mummy or her boy-crazy sister or her oldest sister when she wasn't across the alley working at IBC Biscuits to put food in all their mouths.

Mostly Mummy. Day and night. Her wheezing and choking, dried up lips and starving eyes. Her arms, boned-down fleshless arms, held her in the bedroom with Jesus watching. "You'll be okay. Take deep breaths. A stranger, a madman. You're safe now."

His venom eating her inside out, Jessie wrapped her arms around Mummy, held onto Mummy's ribs at the back. "Don't let them near me. Don't let them touch me."

CECILIA DENISE FED HER in the bedroom, brought the spoon to her youngest daughter's bruised lips. "I'm here. I won't let them in." Terror flit deep and muscular through her daughter's river eyes.

In the dark – her daughter sweating and shaking in her arms, clutching her brittle bones – Cecilia Denise brailed her child's broken skin, felt the burn of his venom running through her child's veins.

"Bring her with you." Jesus' palms throbbed purple in the air-starved bedroom. "She needs you the most."

Cecilia Denise shook her head against the man's poison sinking her and her girl to the bed. "I can't. Go away."

Tears ran down Jesus' face, haggard as her own, down the wallpaper over her head.

"Don't." She sucked in. Panted. "Don't. Cry. For me."

His tears scalded the back of her neck, necklaced her collar-bones sticking out like wings searching for air.

Her own dead mother beside Jesus, tears running out her dark eyes. "*Viens ici*. Both of you. She's poisoned inside out. How can she survive without you? At least you weren't poisoned when I left, until you married that drinking man. And you gave her my name, my own Jessie name. Bring her with you."

Her girl's hot face nuzzled her throat, her bruised lips choked on the tears falling from Cecilia Denise's collarbone. "It hurts, Mummy, I hurt."

"Sssshhhhh." Cecilia Denise ducked her head away from Jesus and her own dead mother. "Time. Just give me. Time."

Through the air-starved night she rocked back and forth on her hands and knees, sucked sharp gasps into her starving lungs, pressed her lips to the wounds in her child's punctured body, until the sun broke the east, and she collapsed beside her girl, panted to her oldest daughter – her speed-skating, barrel-jumping, working girl – "Farm. Take her. To Ivy."

DOUGHY.

Ivy on the farm. One eye aimed sympathy right at Jessie, the other eye roamed wild over the ceiling, the checkered linoleum, the box of yellow chicks warming by the wood stove.

"Maybe after she rests, your mother will recuperate. You can take her a duck egg. Good for building strength, duck eggs." She stepped toward Jessie, stopped, her good eye wet with softness for her. "You can look after these chicks if you want. They need a loving touch with winter coming on."

Trembling for Mummy's fingertips on her raw skin, Jessie followed Ivy's back down a hallway, Ivy's wild eye flicking back at her, jerking away, wide and shocked looking.

Sick with shame for pulling Mummy − hollow-eyed and gasping − up out of her sick-bed, Jessie turned into the wrong room, locked eyes with a snake coiled on the windowsill. Yellow eyes. Unblinking. The head of a pin disappeared into the square of its temple. A high-pitched smell.

I need.

I need my.

Mummy's name on her tongue, she spun into Ivy's thick arms wrapping around her big and pillowing. "Oh, I'm sorry, so sorry. I should have told you. Please don't be frightened. He collects them, my husband. Garters, they're perfectly harmless. The iodine poisons them. That one there's looking for a warm place to die."

PUNCH-DRUNK, Cecilia Denise spun off her husband's fist, floated backward across the room.

Crunch of her spine hitting the wall.

Hollow thunk of her head.

Her husband's eyes red-rimmed, beseeching her, his fat white fists dropped to his sides. "What about me? What about the kids when you're gone? What about us?"

Her girl, her boxing, tap-dancing girl, not there to step between, take his fist, "leave her alone, leave my mother alone."

A child.

Her child.

Safe on Ivy's farm.

On the wall over her bed Jesus lifted his arms. "Come. Come with me now." The howl of bruised flesh. Snapped bones.

"*Maintenant*, Cecile." Light in her mother's black eyes.

Cecilia Denise rolled onto her hands and knees. "Wait. Not. Yet."

THE HIGH-PITCHED STINK OF IODINE.

The high-pitched howl of coyotes.

Jessie fought her eyes open wide, breathed through her mouth past the taste of iodine in the back of her throat.

In her chest, her heart beat Mummy's name.

Who would give Mummy her adrenaline shots to keep her heart beating?

Who would hold her tender enough to make her stay now that Jessie had got her up out of her sick-bed, sapped her strength?

Who would tap-dance a laugh out of her drowning lungs?

Mummy. Miles away across the sun-bleached prairie. Her gasping whisper-voice. "You're a good girl Jess. Not your fault. You remember."

Jessie's eyes dry from fighting her lids. She didn't see him until it was too late, lounging in the shadows two doors down from her own house, his fedora pulled low. She should have been looking.

The way she did in court after the judge banged his gavel and the sick shaking took hold of her. Looked straight into his blue cut-sky eyes aimed right at her from the prisoners' box. "Too bad you missed your chance, kid. When I'm out in five, I'll hunt you down, I'll find you, I'll make you a star."

Shirley Temple. *It's the goo-oo-ood ship lollipop.* At the movies, her curls bounced, she smiled, danced, sang, raised her eyebrows.

His eyes on her, watching her walk toward him.

Her curls.

Her scuffed knees.

Her Mummy too sick to dance, except once, stick-skinny arms and legs flying, breath grunting. *Charleston. Charleston.*

Lounging in the shadows.

In the theatres.

Watching.

PROPPED UP ON HER PILLOWS, her veins on fire, Cecilia Denise mouthed against her oldest daughter's ear. "Bring. Them."

Then she closed her eyes, held the fire in her lungs. Inside the flames of her lids, Jesus beckoned to her. "Now, Cecilia Denise." His voice so soft she could barely hear. Her heart fluttered, shuddered into her ribs.

She moaned. "Wait."

Inside her lids her own dead mother opened her arms wide. "*Viens ici*, Cecile. You can make it."

But they were shuffling in the doorway – seven of her haunt-eyed children.

She smiled. Pointed to the stacks of clothes she had gathered and sewn – checked cowboy shirts, jeans, belts, slips, underwear.

"*Viens ici, Cecile. Une mère aime toujours ses enfants.*"

They huddled inside the door, afraid to touch her, afraid to break her. She could smell their fear, sharp and sweaty.

The weight of the house shifted. Their scared eyes flicked to him, their father, walking in with the wind.

Cecilia Denise put her hand to her chest, caught the shudder of her heart in her palm.

The way her green-eyed girl would.

Her laughing, tap-dancing girl.

The way her own mother would.

Her smiling dark-eyed mother.

A ripping sensation behind her ribs. She clenched her fist around her heart. "Jessie. *Maman*. Hurry."

"Jessie? Jessie?"

Her name on Mummy's panting breath, Jessie opened her eyes. She had closed her eyes without Mummy there, she had let her lids shut.

And there the snake was – coiled around her neck. Warm, heavy, the iodine needle through its temple, staring up at her from her own breastbone. It's yellow lidless eye.

Bile rising in her throat, she grabbed the snake, her own warmth leaking out its muscles, heaved it across the room.

A black hole ripped open inside her. The rust-iron taste of blood.

Mummy. Jesus, Mummy.

She ran past Ivy asleep in her bed, out the door, out into the wind sharp with the taste of snow and grief, into Mummy's whisper voice, a long way across the prairie along the tracks beside the river.

Eleven

BEHIND THE COUCH. MY HANDS OVER MY EARS. He sits on the couch, skunk drunk. "You little bitch," he says, "you wanna smoke, smoke this." Shoves a cigar in my mouth. First he licks it up one side down the other. His tongue is fat. His spit on the cigar. His spit in my mouth. I gag on the cigar shoved against my tongue.

Son-of-a-bitchin' bastard. What kinda father are you anyway? Can't talk with the cigar plugging my mouth.

"Draw," he shouts "goddamned draw." His fat fingers pinch my shoulders. "Jesus Christ you skinny little bitch, suck on the bastard, suck. The way you did the cigarette. I'll teach you to smoke. I'll teach you all right."

Bastard Bastard Bastard.

His eyes watery won't leave me be. Where you come from old man old father old bastard – down by the tracks eh? down by the river eh? drinkin' canned heat with your friends eh? The cigar plugs my mouth. He slaps my cheek. I suck in real cool. My cheek burns.

"C'mon you can do better than that you wanna smoke." His stinkin' breath plugs my nose. I suck on the cigar shoved against the back of my tongue. Swallow swallow swallow stinkin' smoke. Puke in my throat, on my tongue, into the basin.

"Shit," he laughs "shit. You better get used to it cause you're gonna smoke the whole friggin' thing."

"Bitch," he says.

"Bitch bitch bitch." To my mother. His fat fist slams her cheek. She lifts from her chair, dances across the kitchen, hits the wall, slides.

"Fuckin' bitch," he roars, "how can you just sit there dyin', not breathin', what about the kids, what about me when you're dead, what about me?" His hands hang against his green pants. Water runs around his red running drunk nose.

I put her to bed because I am the only one home, half lift, half drag. She is lighter than me and I am eleven friggin' years old.

No
    No Jessie.
    Don't cry,
she grunts from her pillow eyes closed dark brown underneath all around. Bones bones under her thin skin wearing out. Purple bleeds into her cheek.

He
he
doesn't mean
fine man
when sober

HER EYES CLOSED when they carry her out on the stretcher, closed. What about me what about the kids what about me? I stand on the porch as they shove her into the ambulance. Her eyes flicker at him beside the stretcher. My voice screams

I hate
hate
I hate

DOWN

Down by the yards by the tracks, trucks and box-cars all over stinkin' metal. Glass all over broke in the dirt hurts my eyes. Skippin' skippin' down the hill there where he works by the tracks. Sleeves rolled up, suspenders, looks sober at me. "Hey want a pop come sit with your old dad."

The bottle warm in my hands. Warm grape in my throat, up my nose. His fat fingers on my arm. Looks soft green at me. "This here's my little girl." Pats my arm real skinny.

Skippin'

skippin' down the hill by the tracks hot oily where he is. Sits in the glass by the box car

piss drunk the whole lot. Looks hard green at me in the sun. Points a fat finger. "There's a girl who killed her mother."

Pitches his bottle smash into my elbow. Runnin' runnin' up the hill holding my dead arm.

J

J-E
J-E-S-S-I-E Jessie Morris
Doodleeaaahhhtatata

around the kitchen with the mop her hair flying. My sister Elona. Jitter bug jitter bug swing-step. Grabs my hands holds me tight. Angora bounce bounce against my cheek. Her plaid skirt under my fingers.

"Move your feet. Like this."

J-E-S-S-I-E Jessie Morris
Doodleeeaaaahhhhtatata

sings into my hair, my sister Elona. "Mom died, Jessie, you didn't. You're only eleven. You gotta have some fun kiddo."

Around the kitchen her glasses round wire glinty.
"You had

What you said had

nothing to do with her dying"

breathless around the kitchen. *Doodleeeaaaahhhh-tatata*. Smells like lemon. I hold her tight.

"Shush Jessie," she says in the night, hand on my cheek, "shush." My mother's bones click in the black all around. "You know Gabrielle's doing it with her nails. Here, crawl in with me."

Pulls me cold across the dark room click click dancing dead. "Stop that this minute Gabrielle." Her whisper sharp. Pulls me in after her. Quilt up to my ear, my mother's bones loud in the dark. Elona's hand up and down my back.

"Remember, two more months and I'll be twenty-one. Lester and I'll get married and you can come and live with us. I'll be just like mom."

MOM

MUMMY

Elona cries in the night curled on the couch. Fills the sheet Gabrielle and I diaper her in. Crying eyes wide open she doesn't see us. Mummy mummy mummy baby voice. Spit on her chin. "Shush," I say, hand on her head burning up three nights in a row. "Shush."

"Can hardly lift my head," she says first night. Goes upstairs to bed. In the morning moaning head rocking. All day all day cold rags on her temples beating blue under white.

He sits on the couch. "Jesus Jesus Jesus." Shakes his head. "What about me what about the kids?" His fingers in his hair. From upstairs moaning. "Christ," he says and goes out the door.

GABI

Gabi

help me

In the second dark. Shuffle shuffle then Gabrielle's voice across the room. "I'm here Elona. I'm here."

In the lamplight Gabrielle bent over pulling on Elona hunched in her bed. "Gotta peepee gotta peepee."

G-

G-O-

G-O-T-T-G-O-T-T-P-P. I close my eyes. Gabrielle's voice in the double dark. "Come help, Jessie."

Elona's hand curled stiff against her chest. We drag her down thump thump against the steps. My hands clutch her body wringing wet.

G-O-T-T-G-O-T-T-P-P. Her panties bloody on the floor by the toilet. On the can she leans against the wall. "Christ," Gabrielle says, "what a time to get her period. Go call a doctor Jessie. Go call a doctor."

FLYIN' FLYIN' DOWN THE HILL

love love

I love her

to the stars head back screaming. "Please," I beg the operator in the phone booth under stars. "Please," I beg the doctor.

"How old did you say you are? Where did you say you live?"

"Please," I beg.

"Sorry. Too late too far too dirty. Give her an aspirin and put her to bed."

Piss-face Piss-face
Prick
Up the hill. My turn in the fat chair beside the couch. "Mummy." She cries, slobbers in the dark. I stare and stare.

E-

E-L-O

E-L-O-N-A Elona. Around the kitchen, Elona with our dead mother's bones, her hair flying, her glasses round wires glinty. All night.

"No don't, don't," he whispers in the morning, his hands soft on her face, scrunched up eyes rolled white to the ceiling.

I am eleven
eleven friggin' years
old
I have a dead mother. And a dead sister. I live in a shack on a hill outside Calgary. My father lives with me. My brother Jordie lives with me. The others moved away. Every day I make Jordie lard on bread then walk down the coulee across the field to school. In the morning I wear a sweater. In the afternoon I walk with my arms folded over my new tits. More Ass And Tits Than Anyone Else they call me at school. "Your sneakers stink," the home-ec teacher tells me, but they don't. My mother washed them.

Hang up your sneakers on your own back line
And smile smile smile

I sing to my shadow long in front of me. Jordie sits at home eating beans and toast I made him. The grass scratches my ankles. Downtown is a long way along the river along the tracks. "Come and get me at six," he said through the blanket I put up to make a wall for Jordie and me. "You look like your mother. You should've died instead." His fist cracked my skull. That was before the blanket.

It's a long way to Calgary
It's a long way to go

ONE POTATO
Two potato
Three potato
Four
my fingers up the bumps on Loretta Johnson's spine.
Five potato
Six potato
Seven Potato
More
all the way up to the big one on her neck, warm, sleepy, do it again.
One potato
Two potato
down her backbone backbone, ribs ribs.
Counting Loretta Johnson growing tits smaller than mine. "My mom said come sleep at my house."
"What about Jordie?"
"Bring him. He can play with Sam."

At home I tell Jordie, "go get water for the floor."

"Get it yourself."

"Jordie, go get water."

"I said get it yourself."

"You little bugger you little bugger I make your lunch wash your clothes, now you go get water." Pull his hair, my fingers hurt. He dumps water, the whole bucket on the floor. "There." My fist hits his face hard stubborn. "You little bugger."

DON'T SAY SHIT

Don't burp

Don't fart

Jordie's hand sticky in mine across the field. Their house a shack but warm, smells like bread. "Here have some more peas." Mrs. Johnson slides the bowl full green under my nose.

Peas peas peas peas

Eating Johnsons' peas

Goodness how delicious

Eating Johnsons' peas

Stuck to the roof of my mouth, my tongue. Can't say nothing. Jordie across the table, his crewcut hair. "She says thank you." His voice just like the old man's, gravelly and only eight.

"Ain't no Mr. Johnson. Run off a long time ago before Bobbie was born." Loretta whispers under the cover, Jackie and Liz younger across the room. My hands up her pyjamas up and down her back. "What killed your mom?"

One potato
Two potato
"Asthma asthma."
"How'd your sister die?"
Five potato Six potato
"Meningitis on the brain."
Up and down her skinny ribs. "Tell me who you love."
"No, you tell me who you love."
"Never mind tell me tomorrow." Her skin hot sleepy I tingle.
"Promise you'll tell," she murmurs.
Cross my heart
And hope to die
If ever I should
Tell a lie
"Take this with you." Mrs. Johnson tucks a loaf still steaming into my arm. "I always make too much, you come every morning now for bread." At home eat the whole thing lard on.

SEVEN O'CLOCK IN THE MORNING
Skippin' skippin' across the field my belly hungry. Mrs. Johnson puts bread in my arm sometimes tea, lots of milk two sugar. "Come back again before lunch," she says, "a special treat, crusty buns."

C'MON A HEAR
C'mon a hear

Mrs. Johnson's lunchtime bread

I skip out early before lunch, run up the coulee across the field.

C'mon a hear
C'mon a hear
It's the best bread in the land

Push open the door, hear Bobbie crying. "Gotta pee gotta pee."

"No," I shout at Mrs. Johnson on the couch, blue around her lips, fingers stiff around Bobbie's wrist. "No," I whisper to her dead eyes.

"No," I shout and rock Bobbie, pants pissy on my knee.

"What happened what happened?" Loretta runnin' up the hill face scared at the ambulance.

"Nothin'," I say, fingers crossed behind my back, hard.

SOON I WILL BE
    twelve
    twelve friggin' years
    old.

Hand of a Thief

Jessie's thumbs on the girl's throat. Jessie's thumbs, her thick ridged nails, the girl's Adam's apple ridged bone. Jessie's fingers, under the girl's neck, squeeze the girl's spine. Her hands lift the girl's head off the ice. The girl's toque slides sideways, plops to the ice beside Jessie's right knee. Orange.

"You bitch. You goddamned bitch. You sold them, didn't you? Bitch. Bitch. Bitch."

Her hands bang the girl's head into the ice. Her voice in her chest burns.

"Goddamn son-of-a-bitch. You said you're my friend. My friend. My friend."

Her knees rise and fall with the girl's head. Thumbs on the girl's throat, Jessie heaves onto her knees, throws all her weight onto her thumbs. Leans over the girl staring up at her, blue circles under the girl's eyes, blue light of skate blades circling by. Swwiishhhhh sswwiiiissshhhhh. Leans her face into

39

the girl's, close, so close. The girl's lips inches from Jessie's teeth. The girl's Adam's apple cracking under Jessie's thumbs.

EVERY DAY FOR A WEEK the girl comes into the café just as the jockeys pick lettuce and tomato out of their teeth, throw back their fourth cups of coffee, "Can't gain weight, Jessie, gotta stay light, know what I mean," rush out the door, "See ya Jessie kid, keep a steak on ice for me kid, when ya see me sittin' big in the winner's circle, throw 'er on the grill," sprint across Second Street East, through the Stampede Grounds, to the track.

Steam and burgers and onions and mustard and fries and ketchup and vinegar and horses. Horses. Jessie wipes the grey arborite tables, wipes the drips off the ketchup bottles, pockets the dimes and nickels the jockeys hide under their cups.

Warm, she rubs her thumb over their surfaces, breathes deep through her nose. Horses and the sweat of tight-muscled men. Boys, most of them no older than her.

"How old are you, kid?"

"Sixteen."

"Ever waitressed before?"

"Two years at the Kinama Lunch on 17th."

"How old are you really, Jessie?" The owner of the Stampede Grill leans over the counter, looks in her eyes. Grey hair and his eyes soft grey.

"Sixteen in three months."

"Live at home?" His lips hardly move, his eyes soft grey, bags underneath and laugh lines.

Jessie bites her bottom lip. "Liver Lips," the kids at school called her before she left for good, left her books open on her desk, marched beside the river beside the tracks to their shack, hers and Jordie's and their old man's. "Liver Liver Lips." Heat prickles up her neck. She clenches her hands, digs her nails into her palms. Her teeth squeeze her lip inside and out, but she can't, can't stop.

"Jesus Christ," her lip slides free, "Jesus Christ, what's it to you? I want a job. I'm good at what I do, the best goddamned waitress you'll ever find." She spins, marches for the door.

Fuck the rent. Fuck her one-roomer, her hot plate, one mug one spoon one knife one can of beans one mattress too goddamn big for the goddamn bed one buck in her pocket, one lousy buck. Fuck the assholes at school in their new pants and coats and skirts and blouses. "Liver Lips, Liver Liver Lips. Jessie Morris, Jessie Morris, More Ass and Tits than anything else." Fuck Armand and Roy and Walter and Steve and Jordie. Brothers, where the hell are those bastards, and the old bastard, where is he – the Cecil, King Eddy, St. Regis – guzzling canned heat by the tracks? Stay away from me, old bastard, keep your friggin' hands off me. You shoulda kept your filthy hands off my mother.

Jessie marches for the door, heat up the back of her neck. Stares at the wood sign across the road, Welcome to the Calgary Stampede. Wood sign, wood posts, Big 4 building square and brown, and way over by the river, stretched out and floating, horses.

Horses.

Jessie reaches for the doorknob.

"You're hired, kid."

Bangs the knob with her fist. Turns and marches for the apron he holds over the counter, his eyes soft grey watching her.

Grabs the apron, yanks it over her head, "I'll show you what I'm worth, buster," flips the ties around her back. Scoops the pad and pen from beside the till into her pocket, reaches for the grey rag beside the man's hand. "My mother's dead. Don't have a father." Cold, the rag is cold. She squeezes, "This place needs cleaning up. I'll start with the tables by the window."

"Merv," he says, puts out his right hand, "my name's Merv. I got a wife named Peggy, no kids." He turns back to the kitchen, whistles. Whistles all morning. All afternoon. *Lili Marlene, Pack Up Your Troubles, The White Cliffs of Dover.*

Three months now Jessie makes coffee, stacks cups warm from the sink, strides between tables and the order window, swipes the tables clean. The muscles in the backs of her legs, the backs of her arms, along her spine, flow with the sweet sound of Merv whistling. Tighten, relax.

Jessie rings in the jockey's bills, marks down the ones who need credit in the big binder under the counter. Not finished growing and starving themselves.

42

"See you kid." Barney Jenkins straightens his cap, buttons his long grey coat. His hands shake. Jessie wants to say, "What you on, Barney, you taking bennies again?" says instead, "Yeah, see you, Barney. You must be cold-blooded, eh, wearing that big coat this time of year? What you gonna do in a month or two?" "It's a hard life," she says over her shoulder to Merv, "a hard life when you gotta sweat and starve yourself to do your job."

Merv stops whistling. *Peg O'My Heart.* "Most of them are on uppers, kid. Bennies. Watch their hands. But at least they got hands, jobs, at least they were too young to be shipped overseas." Starts whistling where he left off.

"How about you, Merv, you go over?" Jessie holds the salt shakers over a cardboard box, screws their tops off, drops in a few grains of rice, fills the shakers three-quarters full.

By the Light of the Moon. "Nope. Too old." *The Silvery Moon.* "How about your old man, Jessie, he go over?"

A few grains of rice, salt sifting into the shaker, two hard turns on the lid. A deep breath in, she chews on the corner of her lip, blows out. "Missing in action, Merv, he's been missing in action a long long time."

"Hey, Jessie, you so fast you got time to take orders, sling hash, wipe up, and fill the shakers?" Rod McKenzie hands her his bill, slowly shifts a toothpick from one side of his mouth to the other.

"Huh, you should talk about fast." Jessie rings in $1.25. "You eat so fast I can't see your fork, talk so fast

I can't understand a word you say, and I hear you ride so fast your horse can't keep up." She presses the quarter onto the dollar-bill with her thumb, flicks it into the till, slaps the dollar into its slot, snaps the till shut.

"You haven't seen fast yet, wait 'til I get the mount Duncan promised." The toothpick jumps in the corner of his mouth, and his eyes, one looking straight at her right breast, the other somewhere over her left shoulder.

"Go on. Duncan's lying to you. He don't have another horse. Nothing more than's in the stable." Garth Prentiss winks at Jessie, hands her his bill. $1.10 she writes next to his name in the book under the counter. "Don't listen to this guy, Jessie, he's nothing but a two-bit jock. Bet you can smell him from there. Smells like a goddamn horse." He hoists his arm across Rod's shoulders, both of them about her size. "Besides, never believe anyone taller than five-one. Air gets to their brains." He slaps the back of Rod's head.

Jessie crosses her arms over her chest, a year or two or three older than her, tight muscles, cigarettes, horses. Men. Boys. Hair, one swoop like Alan Ladd, pushed back into a wave or blown down over one eye.

"I hear a horse calling your name." She nods toward the track.

"Keep out of the sweat-box," she yells at their backs, one brown bomber jacket, one navy pea, "you're getting too skinny."

"They're getting skinny, Merv," she says over her shoulder, "they're gonna get sick."

Merv whistles one more line. *Auf Wiederseh'n, Sweetheart.* Pokes his head out the order window. "How'd she die, Jess?"

Jessie looks for her reflection in the lid of a salt shaker, finds her face behind all the little holes. Thick lips, and behind them the ridge of gum waiting for her to forget and smile, forget to hold her top lip down, smile and reveal all that wet pink nakedness. Flared nostrils, fierce green eyes. They narrow and jiggle, back and forth. You shoulda died instead, he shouted. Old man old father old bastard. You look like her, you shoulda died instead, his fist flying through the air. Or drunk on Jessie's bed across her legs up her nightie, You look like her, don't leave me don't ever leave me, until Walter with the rifle, Keep your friggin' fingers off her. She's your daughter for Christ sake. All night with the rifle on his lap.

Jessie blows on the lid, wipes with the rag. "Without the old bastard, Merv. Without me."

"Listen, Jess, why don't you come to our house for supper Saturday. Peg, she's a great cook, knows how to warm up to people."

Jessie lays her hands open on the counter, leans into her straight arms. "Thanks, Merv, but I got plans for Saturday. Tell Peg thanks, maybe some other time." She lifts her head, sees smooth honey hair overtop the booth in the corner by the front window. "Jesus, I didn't see or hear her come in. Merv, did you see her come in?" Chop chop from the kitchen, and Merv whistling. *I Don't Want To Set The World On Fire.*

Smooth honey hair. Jessies licks her fingers, runs them through her perm, licks her third finger, smoothes her eyebrows. Across the floor to the corner booth, her heart pounding.

"Hi." Jessie tightens her top lip against her teeth, lets her lips pull back at the corners. "Like a menu?"

Smooth honey hair parted on the side, pulled back in two pink barrettes. "No thanks, I know what I want." The girl smiles up at Jessie. Small coral lips, small teeth, no broad pink wet. And her eyes, dark dark brown. Jessie's top lip trembles. Dark brown, deep brown, smiling at her. Brown-black when Jessie opens her door, sick-bed her mother's sisters called it, your mother's on her sick-bed, opens her mother's door, I need my mother I need my mother I need my mother. Blue-black bruises underneath, all around, on her hands and knees shoulders convulsing, trembling, trying to breathe trying to breathe trying to. Brown-black, smiling at her, arms trembling heart fluttering shoulders shaking wheezing trying to breathe, trying, wraps Jessie in her quilt, rocks her.

you
didn't
do
anything
wrong
some men
just
some
men
oh

Jessie

Jess

Deep deep brown. The girl looks straight up at her, does not blink, her eyes still, thin skin underneath, hint of blue. Jessie's cheeks prickle. Her eyes focus on one of the girl's eyes, then the other. Shards of light, black flecks, around and around, deeper and deeper and deeper. Outside when they sing, outside in the dark when they sing for her dead mother, outside, the sky blue-black and her eyes, her eyes.

Jessie clears her throat, looks across the road across the Stampede Grounds. Two dark shadows float down the track. "Horses," she mutters, "goddamn horses." Looks at the girl still smiling up at her, "You want to order?"

"JESUS CHRIST." In the hallway outside the bathroom, Jessie shifts her weight from one foot to the other, peers down the hall at her closed door. Four times she has come out here, stood with her towel over her shoulder, soap and shampoo in her hands.

Four times. She sighs, takes two steps back toward her room. "To hell with that," spins, balances soap and shampoo on one palm, raps on the door. "If you don't get out of this bathroom in the next five minutes, I'm going to call the police, and if they don't come I'm going to break down this goddamn door and pour every slimy drop of water you're sitting in down your slimy throat."

She slams her door behind her, "Inconsiderate ass–hole, two hours in a shared bathroom. Who the hell do you think you are?" Slides over the hanging end of her mattress, hangs her legs over the edge of the bed, hands shaking. Laid out beside her, her green sweater and brown pleated pants. She strokes the sweater with the back of one hand, her fingertips too rough.

"Green's the colour of leaves and river grass, Jess, they're jealous they don't have green eyes. Here, help me wring out these sheets." Her mother's eyes brown–black in their sockets. Blacker and blacker. The bones in her wrists when she wrings the clothes, her collar bones when the soft spot in her throat caves in wheezing coughing shaking. Black in the night when they carry her out on the stretcher, Jessie on top of the stairs, head back, shouting.

I

      hate

          hate

I hate

Jessie reaches under her bed, slides out a can of tobacco and some papers. One two three, sifts tobacco onto a paper, rolls the paper back and forth, licks the glued edge, presses, tamps the cigarette on her palm, twists one end. Don't think don't think don't think. One two three, flicks a match with her thumbnail, holds the flame in her cupped palm. Breathe in, Sweet Virginia sweet crackle Sweet Jesus, heat in her throat, her lungs.

"Got any brothers and sisters, Jess?"

"You're the nosiest old fart, Merv."

"Just curious, Jess, just curious." His eyes sad grey. He purses his lips, sighs.

"My oldest sister died a year after Mom, Merv. Started with a headache, by night she was burning up. Started baby-talking, couldn't walk. Called the doctor, but he wouldn't come, said put her to bed with an aspirin. She died during the night, crying in a baby voice for Mom. Meningitis, the doctor said. He could've cured her, Merv, but he wouldn't come. No friggin' money."

"Jesus, Jess."

"Yeah, twenty-one years old. She was going to get married, a guy named Lester. He really loved her, Merv, you could tell by the way he listened. They were going to take me and Jordie home with them. After Mom died, Elona'd leave pennies around the house. In drawers, behind jars, on her dresser. Jordie and me took them, bought candy. I was a thief, Merv, stole from my own sister. An ugly no-good thief."

"Jesus, Jess, you were a little kid."

"Yeah, some kid."

Don't think, don't think, don't. Jessie lays her head back, flicks her tongue, flicks out perfect doughnuts floating up to the ceiling.

"I'll come by at seven," the girl said. Her voice soft as her pink cashmere sweater.

"No, don't." Jessie chewed the corner of her bottom lip, how to make her voice less gravelly, how to take the fight out of her voice. "I'll meet you there." The cords in her throat tight, but a shout wanting out – Me, She Likes Me, She Asked Me.

"My name's Laurel." The girl laughed. "Means some kind of tree. Not a nice name-name like yours, Jessie."

Jessie closes her eyes, draws on her smoke, hot and sweet on her tongue, her throat, in her lungs. Holds the sweet burning in her chest.

Mom.

Elona.

In the night, blue-black in the night. Thin skin, bones, him pissed, always pissed. Jordie eight and hanging onto her hand, Don't squeeze so hard, Jordie. In the night, both of them in the night, Elona's hand on their mother's forehead, She can't breathe, Mom can't breathe, get the doctor for Christ sake. Jessie's hand on Elona's head burning up tossing side to side crying for Mom, Don't die Elona, I'll be good, I promise I'll be good.

Laurel.

Some kind of tree.

Some kind of tree.

Jesus, some kind of tree.

JESSIE MAKES HERSELF SLOW DOWN. Her skates, brown speedskates from Walter, Walter walking twenty miles last Christmas from a ranch outside town where he worked, "You're the best damn skater I know, Jess," thump her chest and back, gentle thump through her jacket. Past Dench's truck yards beside the tracks, fresh snow on top of the boxes. Fresh snow on the train cars, the shack where Glen Hubert keeps inventory, where the men go in to warm up between loads.

Jessie laughs out loud. Her muscles warm and ticklish. "Hi Glen," she shouts, though she knows they don't load or unload at night. "You old bugger," she shouts, laughs, spins a circle, her skates spinning around her. "I know what you were up to, you old bugger," she shouts at the empty shack, "you could've sent the broken chocolate back, but you gave it to us because you knew we'd sell it, didn't you? You knew we needed the money for Mom's medicine, didn't you?" Jessie laughs, wipes her eyes with the back of her hand. "I have a new friend, Glen, a friend." Her voice echoes between the cars. "Friend friend friend."

Past the furniture warehouse, square brick in the snow. Run, the muscles in her legs tell her. Run.

She makes her legs take long slow steps toward the Glacier. Snow wets her lashes, melts on her cheeks. She smiles, lets her top lip slide up over her teeth, over her gum. Naked pink in the dark, a cool wind. A friend, I have a friend. She hums, *There'll be bluebirds over the white cliffs of Dover, tomorrow, just you wait and see.*

She arrives before the music starts, slips into the bathroom in the warm-up house, looks for her reflection in the wavy tin mirror over the sink. Same thick lips, flared nostrils, green eyes. She wets her finger, traces her penciled brows, runs Cool Coral over her mouth, mmwwaaa, blots her lips on a piece of toilet paper. A friend, if I don't blow it, if I don't tell too much, if I don't do something wrong. Laurel.

Walks toward her, smiling, a soft pink tam angled on her hair, snow on her lashes. Jessie's hands shake and she wishes she could light a smoke. She yanks the orange toque off her head, shoves it in her pocket, leans against the boards.

"Sorry I'm late, Jessie, I lost track of time." Laurel stops a couple of feet away, smiles. Pink, her lips pink as her sweater, her tam, her cheeks in the falling snow. "You look wonderful, Jessie. You should always wear green."

Jessie hooks her fingernails under her laces, tightens the criss-crosses two at a time up to her ankle. Beside her on the bench, Laurel holds her laces between thumb and finger, pulls slowly. Slowly up her foot, over her ankle. Bent way over, Jessie watches Laurel's fingers, thin and pointed, Laurel's skates, clean white figure skates. Jessie straightens up, clenches her hands into her pockets.

"What kind of skates are those, Jessie? The blades are so long. And look where the boot ends, you don't have any ankle support." Bent over her skates, Laurel smiles up at Jessie. "You must be a good skater." Smooth and shining under the big electric light, Laurel's hair falls across her cheek, cups her chin. "Why don't you go around a few times without me. I don't want to slow you down."

One arm behind her back, Jessie bends over, swings the other, pushes sideways. Glides around the rink, wind in her teeth. Faster and faster. Past Laurel on the bench, her face healthy and shining, watching her, Jessie Morris. One more turn, pumping hard, sweat runs down her back. She stops in front of Laurel, bows.

"You're a beautiful skater, Jessie." Laurel hooks her arm through Jessie's, squeezes her wrist. Jessie's top lip twitches, she tries to tighten it, but it twitches again, glides over her teeth, up and up, cold air and falling snow on her gum. Her hand flies for her mouth.

"No. Don't." Laurel's smooth fingers around her wrist. "Don't cover your mouth, Jess. You have a special smile."

"I NEED A PLACE TO LIVE, JESS." Laurel drops her head over her plate of fries. Her hair swings forward, covers her face.

Jessie grips the pen with one hand, the pad with the other. Laurel's smooth honey hair.

"My dad kicked me out, said he's sick of me coming home all hours, said he doesn't have to put up with a no-good tramp. My mom didn't say anything, just stood there, wouldn't even look at me." Laurel's voice from inside her hair, her hands open beside her plate. She raises a shaking hand, runs her fingers through her hair. "I have no place to go, Jess, no place to sleep. I've been wandering around all day not knowing what to do."

Jessie slides her key across the table, under the edge of Laurel's plate, pulls her hand away fast, "We're pretty busy today," crosses to the far booth. The soft spot in her throat aches.

"You done?" She reaches for a plate, a fork. Wads a napkin, throws it into a glass. The backs of her eyes burn.

"Hey Jess, how is a fast woman like a fast horse?"

Jessie straightens up, looks down at them, boys, three boys, toothpicks in the corners of their mouths.

"I don't want to know." She listens for Merv's whistling in the kitchen. Whistle, Merv, for Christ sake whistle like you do every other goddamn day. She slaps the bill onto the table, "Didn't your teacher tell you whore and horse don't rhyme?"

"Jesus, Jess, can't you take a joke?"

Jessie bangs the plates into a stack, slaps the cutlery on top. "This ain't no joke, boys. This ain't no joke."

OUT OF THE DARK into the dark. Jessie stands still in the foyer, takes a deep breath. Dust, onions, beer, piss.

Slowly up the dark stairway, the soft dip in her throat aches. Slowly down the hallway, hands in her pockets. I did not touch her, did not put my hand on her forehead, did not push her hair away from her eyes. You cannot kill, God, what I did not touch.

Stops in front of her door, thin light underneath. Behind her the floor sighs. She wipes her palms on her sweater, knocks quickly, one two.

"Who is it?" Laurel inside. Laurel her friend, Laurel strong and healthy.

In the dark, Jessie smiles, throws her head back and laughs. "A speedskating waitress." Lets her smile stay wide as the door opens and light frames her in the doorway.

ON HER BACK IN THE DARK, hands tight against her thighs. The radiator clicks, hisses. Jessie clenches the muscles in her left shoulder, arm, buttock, keeps from sliding down the mattress hanging over her side of the bed.

"Did you ever have a boyfriend, Jess?"

Jessie turns her face toward Laurel's voice, feels Laurel's eyes watching her in the dark. "Kind of."

Laurel laughs, softly. "What do you mean, kind of?"

Jessie closes her eyes. The Elbow River, the boy on his bike ahead of her, rocks and grass under her tires and she leans over her handlebars, pumps, her front tire beside his back tire, turning into, nudging. Crazy, he shouts over his shoulder, his bike flying off the bank, you're crazy Morris. Her bike flying, arcing, splash into the river, her arm locked around his neck, dunks his head underwater, pulls him up, kisses him wet on his cold wet mouth. Liver Lips. Liver Liver Lips. The back of Jessie's neck prickles.

"Come on, Jess, I want to hear."

Jessie's cheeks burn in the dark. "Why?"

"Because we're friends. I want to know everything about you."

"You can't know everything."

"Why not?"

"Because I can't tell everything."

"Why not, Jess, why can't you tell me everything?" Laurel shifts closer, her breath on Jessie's cheek.

Jessie clenches and unclenches her hands. "There isn't time."

"Of course there's time, Jess. Years of time. Friends last years and years." Her hand reaches for Jessie's shoulder.

Jessie flinches. "Don't."

Laurel's hand smooth on her shoulder. "I like you, Jess, I want to be your friend."

"THIEF. You goddamn lying thief."

The girl's lips puffy and blue. Flash of blue light, blue skate blades. "She stole my skates," Jessie yells as they hoist under her arms, pry her fingers from the girl's throat, "she stole my clothes, she stole my skates."

"Get your friggin' fingers off me," she yells as they drag her, back arched, heels banging, across the rink, "I've had enough of people fucking touching me, lifting my stuff."

"I trusted her," she yells, head back to the stars as the girl stands, brushes off her brown pleated pants, her green sweater, skates straight for Jessie held up against the boards.

"Goddamn friggin' trust," Jessie yells as the girl's picks aim for her right thigh.

Rosalind

Upstairs

I DON'T REMEMBER WALKING BESIDE MY MOM to the green store in Bridgeland when we lived downstairs from Detlev and Monika and their mom, Peṭa, and their dad, Gustav, and Detlev was a baby but he could crawl across the grass, sun on his big round head. One time Peta brought a stuffed lung down to us, hot and steaming and smelling sweet and spicy in a glass dish, and my dad who worked in a meat packing plant went white and sweaty around his mouth, said he could bring them lungs anytime, they got thrown out with the guts, and we tried brain and tongue and heart, and his bosses put him on the killing floor once, my dad, but he couldn't do it, stood with the stun-gun to the steer's temple, looking in its eyes, until the steer bawled at him, chased him up the pen, grabbed him by the side with its big yellow teeth.

AND I DON'T REMEMBER, because I wasn't old enough to know what they meant, Detlev and Monika's mom and dad, Peta and Gustav, telling my mom that Gustav fought against the Nazis in Germany where they came from, joined the forces against Hitler, and how Gustav's father kept a wireless radio under the bed listening to the Gestapo, this was how his father found out they'd been betrayed by a neighbour and when the car pulled up in front of their house and the Nazi soldiers got out, Gustav's father hanged himself in the stairway while Gustav and Peta were on their way to Canada, Calgary, Bridgeland, Upstairs.

AND I DON'T REMEMBER walking beside my mom, sun hot on the top of my head, my doll tucked safe in the buggy I was pushing, a wicker buggy, not like the blue buggy Mummy was pushing, blue hood and springs and it bounced and the springs rattled and my new baby sister fast asleep. I don't remember lying in bed crying when my mom left to go have the new baby, shaking and wanting her to come and pick me up, "Don't cry, Rozzie , I'm not leaving you," wanting her hand on my forehead. Or standing at the top of the three steps down to the porch when she came in with the new baby wrapped in a thin blanket and the new baby started squirming and crying and I didn't know babies cried, didn't know they weren't like dolls, dolls you just lay back and their eyes clicked shut, but this baby filled the whole porch with her squirming and crying and I don't remember shaking my head, "You better take her back where you got her from."

Except now she has a name, Celeste, and I can't stop kissing her cheeks, sniffing her neck, her belly button, the bottoms of her feet, staring into her eyes when my mom lays her on the table to change her diaper and Celeste's eyes move dark and slow around the room and I stand on a chair, lean my tummy against the table edge, lean over her and touch my lips to her lips, so small and her top lip has a hard spot where it dips down and my mom says, "Stop kissing her on the mouth all the time. Here, why don't you kiss the cord on her belly button, see if you can make it fall off faster." And I do, rubbing-alcohol taste on the stiff cord, kiss of a sister for all the fist-fights, poverty, sleepless nights, abusive men, fast jokes, rub my back in the dark, growth of breasts for god's sake, blood-loyal thick years ahead.

I DON'T REMEMBER, because it happened before I was born, but I can taste the cabbage and tomatoes and spiced meat, the sweet irony of another refugee couple, an Italian woman and her Polish husband and their two little girls, taking my Canadian-born mother into their home, teaching her, a skinny kid on her own at thirteen just after the war, how to open a bank account and how to cook the dishes they ate on weekends at the homes of other refugees, made her feel at home, kissed her goodbye when they had another baby and she left knowing how to cook and bank and welcome people in. Detlev on the grass, sun on his round head, my baby sister on her tummy on a blanket, my mother puts her arms around Peta and Gustav, they wipe their eyes with the backs of their hands.

MONIKA, BEAUTIFUL MONIKA, at five or six so tall beside me in the yard. I am four and love to look up at Monika, the sun in her dark hair. She tells me there's a baby in her church, baby Jesus, would I like to see him, and I do, want to kiss him the way I do my baby sister. There in the yard, then outside, the gate shut behind us, heading down the street toward her church, I can smell him already, baby Jesus, I've never met him, but I'll hold him, sniff him, kiss him, like Celeste or Detlev, but my Mom's voice breaks the summer air, breaks into my running breath. High and loud, "You get back here this minute." We stop. "Tell her be quiet, you old bitch," Monika says. I do. Turn around and yell, "Be quiet, you old bitch." I remember the taste of Dove soap in my mouth, vomiting bubbles, my mother's voice, "Don't ever speak to me that way again."

SHE DOESN'T CRY or even open her eyes, my baby sister, when the buggy bounces, and I can't wait until we have finished shopping and are home and my mom lays Celeste on the bed and I can help undo the blanket and pull up her nightie and run my fingers over her velvety legs and I even love the smell of pee. "Here," my mom says, "you can bring your doll-buggy inside," and she opens the door. I push my doll-buggy under her arm, into the cool and the smell of marshmallows I can taste. She pulls Celeste's buggy in backwards, then starts pushing it up and down the aisles, picks up cans and boxes, lays them softly around Celeste in the buggy. Okay, I think, I better shop for my baby, too. So I find my own aisle, pick up a box of Lucky Elephant Popcorn, imagine the pink taste in my mouth, a box of animal crackers, mmmmm hmmmmmm, a licorice cigar, the kind with red candy beads on the end, tuck them under the edges of my doll-baby's blanket, right up against her shiny skin. My mom stops where the ladies stand at the machine that rings and clinks, puts all her things on the counter, but I am too busy shopping. A bag of coloured marshmallows, soft as the skin on Celeste's tummy. A chocolate bar – I sniff first, sweet and chocolaty through the wrapper. Then my mom is at the door, two paper bags propped at the end of Celeste's buggy, where Celeste's feet can't begin to reach, "Let's go Rozzie, time to go feed the baby."

I AM REMEMBERING my mother's memory – long before she had me, before she was eleven and picked up by a stranger at the end of their block here in Calgary, across the river, the tracks, dragged along the railway, beaten, bitten, violated, left for dead, got her mother up out of her sick bed where she died three weeks later and the little girl who became my mother thought she caused her mother's death, then her oldest sister, the speedskating, archery strong sister, died of meningitis in the night crying in a baby voice and the doctor wouldn't come because they couldn't pay him. Before that, before her dad beat the shit out of her and her dying mother and the other kids. Before all of that, I remember her sitting on her mother's knee, stroking her mother's face, pushing her fingers into her mother's mouth, fingering the toothless bottom gum, her whole yet-unremembered life ahead of her, the four children she loves with the passion she is devoting to her mother, right here in the kitchen, now.

AT HOME SHE PULLS HER BOXES and packages and cans out of the two brown bags, shoves them into cupboards. I pull out my lucky Elephant first, rip open the top, sniff that pink, my mouth waters. Then the licorice cigar, hold it in my mouth while I slide animal crackers and chocolate bars and marshmallows out from under the blanket in my buggy, arrange them around the edges of the table, so I can reach them when I need to. At last she's ready to lay Celeste in the middle of the table, in the centre of all my groceries. She leans, one arm around Celeste's back, the other around Celeste's floppy neck, stops, looks at my groceries, looks at me. "When did you get these?" "I shopped them, when you were shopping." The corners of her mouth twitch and her eyebrows move up and down. "I think we better go back. You have to pay for things you put in your buggy. If you don't pay it's called stealing." I don't remember her laying Celeste back in her buggy, helping me put my popcorn and marshmallows and chocolate bars back under the blanket in my buggy. I don't remember the walk back to the store, past the gardens and flowers onto the big street with cars, the green store on the corner, the buggy springs squeaking. I don't remember telling the ladies at the machine that I stole all my groceries and I was sorry, I wouldn't do it again, but could I keep one thing, and they said, "Sure you can, honey, for being honest," and oh the soft pink taste of Lucky Elephant.

WE MAKE ANOTHER RUN FOR IT, Monika and I, make the corner, the hill, the church. At home my father arrives from the meatpacking plant, runs through the open gate, into the kitchen where my mother is changing Celeste's diaper, his face white and sweaty, "where's Rozzie? I just heard on the car radio that the police found the body of a little girl beside the river. They said a man is stealing little girls from their yards in Bridgeland." While my mom phones the police, Monika and I sit under the blue stained glass baby Jesus gluing cotton batting onto popsicle sticks, and I am sick that Jesus is up there in the blue glass away from my arms and lips. We hear the siren split the spring air outside. Shivering,

Monika and I slide under the table, watch our parents
race down the stairs ahead of the police to where we
are and cool blue light kisses their faces.

Tunnels

"The Pass," we say when we talk among ourselves, those of us who live or have lived in
this river valley, slept and loved and keened
and danced below the deep green and stark grey
mountains all around. "The Pass," we say, the methane
taste of mine on our tongues, undulating folds of
earth and rock under our skin, evergreen and aspen in
the air we breathe.

"The Crowsnest Pass," we say to people who may
or may not have driven through the Frank Slide,
miles of sheer-faced boulders spread across the valley.
We search for words to describe living next to 90
million tons of fractured rock, to articulate the way
mountains wear time, silk-sacked or cut loose in the
wind, so much wind blowing through curves and
clefts, stings our eyes when we walk uptown, when
we huddle outside the mine's mouth, time dank and
sour and cold on our breath, waiting.

"YOU HAVE A PENCHANT FOR TRAGEDY," my friends say. I bring them here from the city. We walk up and down the long mass grave in Hillcrest at the foot of Turtle Mountain. The mountain broods over our shoulders. We read the gravestones. June 19, 1914. June 19, 1914. 189 men and boys killed on the same day, same explosion. Just weeks before the start of World War I.

My husband and I climb a shoulder of Turtle Mountain, to the highest peak. To the west the rocky peaks of the Andy Good Range look purple in the mountain haze. We crawl on our stomachs out onto the boulder hanging over the edge of the slide, stare two thousand dizzy feet straight down onto the limestone slide fanned out below us. "Hold my ankles," I ask my husband, the urge to fly tingling up my back, into my arms. With the tips of my fingers I trace the fossils embedded in the rock, shells and tubes and coils. Trace the shapes of the bodies buried under rock, curled or half sitting in their beds.

WE HAVE NOT MOVED THERE, yet, to the Crowsnest Pass, the place our dad lived when he was a boy, rode horses in the mountains, his hands wrapped in his mare's sorrel mane. He rides uphill, toward the rocky ridge that separates his village, Bellevue, from the flat world to the east. His mare's hooves kick up dust along the mine road, swish through grass across mountain meadows.

Deep in the earth beneath them, miles of twisted tunnels dug and blasted from down beside the river, up into the veins of coal running inside the mountain. His father, fire boss in the Bellevue mine, trudges through those tunnels, somewhere down there in the dark and damp, measuring levels of methane gas, marking them on pillars.

In their shack in Bogush's field, the wind howling through the spaces between wallboards, his mother takes a snifter of rye whisky, peels potatoes and carrots and arranges them with onions and chicken and salt and pepper in the clay pot she brought from Wales, first to Saskatchewan, alone with three babies on the prairie, the nearest neighbour miles away, then here to these brooding mountains. When her husband gets home, coal-eyed and quiet, she'll snatch his glasses off his face, slap him hard. A boxing miner, he'll try to hit her back. They rip at each other's clothes, throw fists, until one of the children run for the police officer.

In the meadow up the mountain behind Bellevue, the youngest child leans over his mare's neck, her muscles warm and rhythmic under his skin. The day before he and his brothers and sister and parents move to the city, he rides her out into the mountain behind Bellevue, slides the hackamore off her head, turns and walks away. The road shimmers and a hole opens in the middle of his chest, a deep hunger for mountains, even as he walks among them.

SO SHY THE ONLY EYES HE CAN LOOK INTO are a horse's, the velvety cones deep inside, at 16 he joins his brother, a trainer on the Calgary Thoroughbred track, pops Bennies that make him vibrate and kill his appetite, eats scraps of others' leftovers, seals his melting body in a sweat box. An apprentice jockey, he gallops the long-legged Thoroughbreds around the track, dust and wind in his eyes.

Across from the track my mother, 15 and on her own since she was 13, slings hash, hamburger, fries, cooks up double batches of pancakes, pours coffee for the trackies and truckers in the Stampede Grill, open 24 hours except Sunday. She is wiry and fierce, laughs or dances or throws a punch or hugs a crying man or woman as fast as she can pour a cup of coffee. At nights she rocks herself to sleep in her boardinghouse room, longs for her mother who died when she was 11, years of gasping and coughing and wheezing, especially when the horses came back in the spring to the track down the street, until one night the main aorta ripped away from her heart. "Her heart exploded," the doctor explained. "That can happen – too many years of struggling to breathe and the heart explodes."

Off-shift, my mother goes over to the track, walks the hots, sweating and steaming after their gallops. She holds their halters close to her shoulder, talks to them, laughs when they nuzzle or butt her.

At the Stampede Grill, early in the morning, fried onions and eggs and toast in the air, she walks round the counter, looks out the window at a couple of trackies crossing the road. The older one she knows, the younger dark-haired boy with clear hazel eyes she doesn't. A sharp pain pierces her belly. Sick, she thinks, flu or appendicitis.

In their one-room apartment where their plates in the cupboard explode at night and they laugh until they cry — she, because this shy, smart boy, with his quiet ways and a singing voice that makes her weep is here, he, because this unpredictable girl with her wild eyes and capable hands can reach through the shyness inside him — she tells him that she's pregnant but doesn't expect him to stay behind. He gets up from the bed, walks through a July morning down to the traintracks, spends the day loading the horses on the boxcars for Toronto, tells the other jocks goodbye, walks back to their apartment.

HE BRINGS US to the Crowsnest Pass for the first visit I remember when I am six, my sister two. He comes home from Burns Meat Packing Plant where he cuts meat all day, says to our mom "I want to take you to the mountains. We need to get out of here." My sister and I sniff his hands, his neck, that meaty blood smell.

We drive at night, from Calgary to the Crowsnest Pass, one hundred and twenty miles across prairie, through dark mounded foothills, into mountains, the smell of sweet grass turning to aspen to spruce to limestone. "You're going to stay with Mr. and Mrs. O," our mom and dad tell us, "just for a few days."

They drop us off in Bellevue, at Mr. and Mrs. O's tiny brown house, then disappear into the mountains on horses.

Celeste and I stand in the back yard, stare across the valley at Turtle Mountain's face, gouged and grey. Lean into the wire mesh fence, smell horses on the wind. Hot and oaty and sweet.

We follow Mrs. O around the yard, her black sweater over a dark flowered dress, a babushka over her hair. She kneels between rows of carrots and peas, "This is a weed. This is what you pull." Her square fingers gently pull the weeds from the earth. Celeste and I squat beside her. We have one grandmother, our dad's mother, she is wild and impatient, her black hair curled, lipstick around her red mouth, her black eyes far away. We put our chubby hands beside Mrs. O's, our fat fingers try to mimic hers. She grabs a feathery plume, picks a carrot, wipes it on her apron. "Come eat." She holds the carrot up to Celeste's mouth, her other hand gentle under Celeste's chin. Celeste stares at Mrs. O, her eyes dark and solemn. She opens her lips, crunches her sharp baby teeth into the carrot's flesh. She chews, her lips closed.

"Now your turn." Mrs. O holds the carrot to me, touches her fingers under my chin. The smell of carrots and earth, and Mrs. O's fingers hanging sour milk in the sun, wringing whey through cheesecloth, kneading sweet pastry dough warm and fragrant in the tiny kitchen where she will stuff it with apples and prunes and bake it in the coal stove. She combs our wild hair before bed, tucks us under the fat quilt she tells us is full of feathers she plucked from her own chickens.

One morning, the sun rising above the mountain behind the Os' house, Celeste and I are out in the yard, watching the chickens peck at the ground, at each other. I have dressed us in the white cotton shirts our mummy bought us, little girl's faces embroidered on the front, real braids made out of yellow wool. Mrs. O walks across the yard toward us, fast. She is not watching the chickens, she is watching me and Celeste. She stops in front of me, kneels, strokes the girl's face and yellow braids, her hand warm on my pot belly. Then she pulls us close, holds our faces pressed to her chest.

When she lets go, her eyes are round and red. "Just like you," she says, smoothing the wool braids against my tummy, "In Europe I had two daughters just like you and your sister. During the war they were starving, we ate grass, they swelled up and died." She strokes the braids against my tummy.

I AM OUT IN THE YARD with the chickens. Buck-buckbuck buckuuuuck. Light dizzy on Turtle Mountain's missing face, darkness in the pines up the hill, my mom and dad riding in those mountains on horseback, away from us.

The chickens are reddy brown with red rubbery fingers on their heads that wiggle and shake as they peck at the ground. The smell of pines, taste of pines, on the soft back of my tongue. Here chuck chuck chuck chuck. The humps on top of Turtle Mountain, the sensation of falling when I stare at Turtle's gouged face. Very still in the yard, my hand out to the chickens. Here chuck chuck chuck.

The rooster flies at me, his neck flaming, beak wide open, aims for my eye.

Mrs. O's skirt swishes my cheek, she grabs the rooster mid-air, twists his neck. She marches back into the house, the rooster's head bobbing upside down.

MR. O HOLDS MY HAND up the mine hoist road. Our feet clomp, lift puffs of dirt. We leave the road, step high through bush, over dark rocks, into the cool shade of evergreens and poplar. Mr. O lets go of my hand, bends, snaps a mushroom stem. "This kind you eat, a little butter, little garlic." He holds the mushroom upside down on his palm, riffles the fleshy gills under the cap. "Some kinds, one bite and you die, but this kind is very good." He holds the mushroom out to me. I squeeze the stem, cool and smooth, run my finger over the gills, sniff. Cool and earthy. Lay it gently in the basket hanging from my arm.

Snap, fleshy snap. Mushroom after mushroom. In the cool shade, sweet poplar leaves wet against our legs, up the hill, the moist taste of earth and pine and limestone in the back of my mouth.

The cold wind seeping out of the black hole in the hill. He points, "Your grandfather worked in this mine." He walks off into the bush to pee. I stare into the black dank gash in the rocks.

I AM SEVEN. We still live in Calgary. We have moved out of our rental house into my aunt's and uncle's basement. My mom and my little sister and baby brother and the new baby in my mother's belly.

"A side of beef fell on him," she told me when my dad didn't come home from work and she started packing boxes, "crushed his hard-hat, ripped the cartilage in his knee."

"Crushed his heart-hat," I tell a friend in my new school, my finger on my chest, "it's to protect your heart. It worked. His heart's okay, but he needs a knee operation."

"He's out hunting for food for the family," my mother tells the man from the service-station who phones back after she applies for a job for my dad who's still in the hospital in another city. "In the hospital," she tells the man when he phones back to say he can't wait, "my husband's smart, a damn hard worker, we have four kids to feed. Give him a chance and you won't be sorry."

I AM EIGHT. We have just moved out of our aunt's and uncle's basement into a rental house in an old part of the city.

"A pump-jockey" my dad jokes, "I used to be a jockey, now I'm a pump-jockey." He wears a grey uniform with a cap. That's him in the photo, hands on his hips, squinting into the sun in front of the rental house with lilacs beside the front door and holes in the walls upstairs my sister Celeste and I put our hands through, wrap our fingers around our little brother Alyd's throat, his heart fast as a baby bird's.

At school the teachers tell us there are missiles aimed at Calgary, give us brochures to take home that have targets on them. We watch films about atomic bombs, a flash of white light that blinds you and melts your skin, erupts into a mushroom cloud that blasts to bits everything near it. We learn about radiation sickness where you are too dizzy to stand and cannot stop throwing up. A boy in my class says that happened to some of his family in Japan.

Everyday the fire bell rings at school and we have to drop onto the floor on our faces, cover the backs of our necks with our hands or a book. The alarm jolts me, shocks zap through my body. I press my forehead into the floor, wait for the flash of white light.

At lunch the school bell alarms us into running home, where our mothers are supposed to time how long it takes us to reach the safety of their arms. I am small and scrawny, but can run fast, wind in my teeth, the taste of my heart in my throat sour and electric.

At night I lie in my bed upstairs in the room with Alyd and Celeste. Every time I close my eyes, there is the blinding flash, Mrs. O's daughters' faces like the children in the newsreels we see from the second world war with their haunted eyes and sunken cheeks, Gustav's father swinging in the stairwell while the Gestapo push open his front door.

Every night I lay my blankets on the floor under my bed where the Nazis can't find us, bring Alyd and Celeste to lie with me. "Sssshhh," I tell them, "we are playing hide and seek, and have to be very quiet."

In the evenings my mom phones my dad at the service station and asks him to talk to me. "Rozzie," he says, "that was the second world war. All that stuff at school is practice."

"Dad, there are missiles aimed right at us."

"Roz, when it's time to hide under the bed, we will let you know."

"It's too late then, Dad."

And he's right, my dad. The Nazis don't come in the night.

I'm flying home, icy wind in my throat, my eyes. Crunching over snow, trying to catch up with my shadow. Toward home, my mom's strong arms and lunch, Celeste who is only five but can sing in tune and remembers the words for all the songs we sing together. We will sit down after lunch, and my voice will loop and swirl around hers, and Alyd who is three, wide blue eyes and halo of white hair like he's always surprised, will interrupt us, "what if the house falls over when we're all upstairs?" "What if the big trucks on the road drive up onto the sidewalk when we're walking?" "What if lightning hits the house and makes a ball that crashes down the chimney?" Celeste and I will get him to sing with us, and their round faces and voices and the chicken noodle smell of them will melt the knot of worry in my belly.

I fly in the front door.

Almost step on Celeste's troll doll with the pudgy cheeks and flaming pink hair that Celeste likes to tickle under my chin and speak through in a gruff voice, "you forgot to take your leotards off."

The electric shocks starting up inside, I scan the living room for Alyd, even though I can see he is not there playing with the blocks he builds houses with to keep out lightning and paving trucks.

"Mom?" I run through the living room into the kitchen.

A half cup of coffee, my mom's lipstick lip print. Half-eaten toast. Alyd and Celeste's special drink cups.

"Mommy? Celeste? Alyd? Where are you? Where are you?" My voice is high and shrill and my yellow canary Dickey starts to sing.

I tear up the stairs. "Mommy? Mommy?" Into the little room with the holes in the wall and the naked light bulb. My voice echoes back at me from the emptiness. Downstairs Dickey stops singing. Into our bedroom, the beds still unmade. "Mommy?" Into my mom's and dad's bedroom, their blankets and bedspread in a heap.

I stand in the middle of my parents' bedroom unable to breathe.

I take Celeste's troll doll, one of Alyd's blocks, consider taking Dickey, but it is snowing out and windy. Alyd's block in my pocket, Celeste's doll tucked inside my shirt beneath my chin, I crawl under the back porch. A car pulls up in front of our house. My dad walks toward the porch in his service station uniform. Shivering and gulping, I throw myself into his arms and cannot stop crying into the warm front of his jacket.

He rubs the top of my head, the back of my neck. "Celeste and Alyd are next door. Mommy's gone to the hospital to have the new baby. "

A woman comes in to cook, and my bird Dickey dies. I will not eat because I know she's a Nazi spy and is poisoning our food. I don't tell my dad. I insist on boiled eggs for breakfast and lunch and supper. "You can make them, Daddy," I tell him, "and so can I. We don't need her to cook for us."

We have a new baby now, Gareth. We call him Captain Huff and Puff because he huffs and puffs and laughs when we talk to him.

He's not laughing now. "Dying," the doctor says to my mom in the front room where our baby lies in his crib, his stomach caved into his backbone, his skin dry and burning, the lump in his neck that's killing him swollen an angry red.

We cry, all of us, including my aunt and uncle who have come over to see him. Upstairs the walls cry, the holes in the walls, the peeling paper. My stomach feels sick and I keep getting up in the night, touch my little sister's and brother's faces.

"He's getting better," my mom tells me when she comes home from the hospital where she's been sleeping beside our baby's crib. "It was an abscess. The doctor had only seen one like it. He lanced it." She hugs me. "He lanced it and saved Huff and Puff's life."

He leaves in the morning or afternoon or before bed, my dad, to go pump-jockey. "He's learning to talk to people more," my mom tells me. "His boss likes him and he likes his boss." Captain Huff and Puff comes home, stands up and walks at ten months, carries around a book, *I Know a Secret*, upside down. We turn it right-side up, but he gives us a look and turns it back upside down.

A dead deer hangs upside down in our basement, its eyes empty, its wild smell filling our nostrils. "He had to shoot it," my mom tells me. "How else can we eat?"

They whisper, my mom and dad, about not having enough money. How can we pay the rent? How can we feed four kids? They're cutting the water off. What the hell can we do?

In school I write an essay about my mom, win an airplane ride for her and me on Mothers' Day. All spring I imagine how it will be flying over the city she grew up in, her green eyes flashing.

A month before Mothers' Day she tells me in the kitchen, "We're moving to the Crowsnest Pass." Her green eyes flicker.

I throw myself on the floor, bang my forehead into the black and white squares, "I'm not moving there, they take canaries down the mine and they die, they take ponies down and they go blind." Black and white squares slam up to meet me. My head aches, but I can't stop. "I'm not moving there. Mountains fall on people, kids drown in the river, wood ticks jump out of trees and paralyze you." I pound my fists, my head, my feet into the floor, black and white, black and white.

She puts her hand on my back, "I'm proud of you and I want that airplane ride as much as you do, but Daddy has a job offer there cutting meat again. That's the day we move."

But I can't stop banging my head into the floor, until she phones the doctor, "She's hurting herself and I can't stop her," and he tells her to throw a glass of cold water in my face.

Hunched in the backseat of the car on Mothers' Day, our belongings piled onto an open trailer behind us, I listen to the drone of a small plane, imagine my friend and her mother up there watching us drive away from this city into the mountains.

CELESTE AND I STAND ON THE CLIFF behind the tiny grey rented house we have just moved into, with our mom and dad and two little brothers, at the edge of Bellevue, Turtle Mountain humped and brooding across the valley, the river green and glinting way below. Up river, the square jaws of the mine open out of rock. A steady gush of water spews out of the mine, rusty and stinking of rotten eggs.

Down we go, straight down the cliff, our feet finding wedges and fissures, our bodies upright. Turtle Mountain grows taller, darker. We jump into shale at the bottom of the cliff, kneel on the railway tracks, "Put your hand here, Celeste, you can feel a train coming." We lay our hands on the hot metal, sniff creosote and tar.

We leap the tracks, run for the river. We stop where the tree hangs over, where the water has a dark voice, where the trout flit. The water's deep here, way over our heads. We hold our hands underwater until our wrists turn numb. Squat on the edge, over the bottomless green pool.

"What if I fell in?"

"You'd drown."

"I feel like falling in. I feel like doing a somersault right in. I want to be a fish."

EVERY MORNING a girl with red hair and silvery-sage eyes calls on me, sun just coming over the ridge. Walks with me up the dirt road in front of our house, across the highway, along the winding streets at the edge of town, past Fidenato's & DeCelia's big red store, across the field toward M.D. McEachern Elementary, low and red brick. Walks with me through the light slanting over the ridge, our shadows along the grass beside us. I look at the ridge, the grass trees sky mountains, and shiver, laugh, fall silent.

The same girl walks home with me in the afternoons. We sit outside in my backyard, amidst glacial gravel and hulking boulders, and she brushes my hair, long strokes down my back to my waist, while I stare at Turtle Mountain.

On summer afternoons, her hair tied back in a thin red ponytail, she calls on me and we running-shoe down the cliff, walk upriver along the tracks, climb the mountain of coal beside the Bellevue mine. The mine closed down the year before we moved here, but the slag heap is still here. So is the towering tipple where miners washed and sorted coal and loaded it onto train cars. So are the shacks and wooden mine cars and heaps of rusty metal and broken glass.

We can smell the mine's mouth, cold rotten eggs, from way up here on our mountain of coal. We yell, race for the edge, coal crunching under our feet, arms and legs pumping, wind whipping our hair. We yell, throw ourselves over.

"Jesus Christ," my mom says, the comb wedged between a lump of coal and my scalp, "what the hell were you doing?" She yanks, "I can't get it out. It's wrapped to your skull." The friend who combs my hair sits in a chair across the table. My mom picks up the scissors. Hair and coal fall to the floor. My friend does not wipe her tears, does not look away.

THE HOOF-BEATS OF A HORSE. Smell of horse, hot and sweaty.

Dark bay, head stretched forward, nostrils quivering, a girl leaning over its neck, a horse gallops all muscle and shine along our wire fence, spins toward the fence, rears and snorts.

The horse tosses its head, dances sideways, makes little grunting sounds. The girl sits loose in the saddle, stares at me. I stare back at her. Tall and muscled.

My eyes already beginning to itch and burn, I turn to my mom who is stroking the horse's sweated neck.

"Rosalind needs to eat first." My mom's pats the horse's chest. "Why don't you tie your horse to the fence and come in for lunch?"

"I can't come in your house."

My mom looks up. "What's wrong with our house?"

"I can't come into your house because I'm Indian."

"Your dad and Rosalind's dad used to ride together up in the mountains when they were boys." My mom turns and walks toward the house. "If you can't come into our house, Rosalind can't come riding with you."

All summer I sit behind Hazel, hold onto her waist or the back of her saddle, the flex and surge of her horse's flanks under my legs and buttocks, up the mountain behind her house where our dads rode as boys, a full gallop through meadows, the cool shadows of cliffs, aspen leaves fluttering in the wind, a deep love for these mountains opening inside, a hunger for horses.

My eyes swell and burn and I cannot stop sneezing, but I do not tell her that, when I was five and my eyes swelled and burned and I could not breathe after my dad took me to the track, the doctor injected my arm with a serum from a pregnant mare, only once-in-a-lifetime the doctor told my parents, it's so potent. My arm swelled twice its size. Horse blood from my father's side, generations of Welsh men breathing horse. Blood from my mother's, two generations of French women stopped breathing in their forties because of horses. Flowing together in my veins. Would I wake up a horse, I wondered, and if I did, would I be allergic to myself?

And Hazel does not tell me that her grandfather rode horses into these mountains, pastured them here in the summers, before white people and mining companies and lying government agents put up fences, stole the land, dug tunnels into the mountains' veins.

We talk about where we rode today. Listen to the horses breathing. Watch the mountains disappear into the night sky.

Sun loud in the sky, on my neck, Turtle Mountain brooding across the valley. New leaves on the trees and the wind, always the wind here in these mountains. The crunch of coal under my feet, rocks in this barbed-wire wildness at the edge of town, this tiny grey house perched on the edge of a cliff, the shed dark and lonely at the back of the yard.

And a colt. A rearing black colt. Sun in his coat, sun in my dad's black hair. "Easy boy, easy," my dad croons, waits until the colt's feet touch the ground, slowly raises his hand, strokes the colt's neck. "Easy boy, easy."

He turns, hands the halter rope to me. "Here, take him, he's yours. I got him up in the mountains. He's wild, but you can help train him."

Four months later, aspen leaves flaming the mountains brilliant yellow, we buy a house in town, above the Bellevue mine, for $2,700. The people selling the house are from Holland. They loan us money so we can buy their house. We pay them as if we are renting, no interest.

Celeste and I climb the two giant poplars in the backyard, run around and around the huge lawn. I perch my baby brother on a low branch so I can take his picture. As I am looking through the view-finder, he begins to sway back and forth. "Sit still," I tell him, as he flips backward out of the tree.

The house stinks of sewer and our skin turns yellow. We keep the windows open. We walk around queasy. A man comes with a truck and pumps out the cesspool in our backyard, but the stink rises damp and sickening through all the rooms. One day our dad takes a pick-ax into the dug-out basement, aims it at a cement block against the wall. Sewer geysers out. "Jesus," he yells, "some asshole put a cesspool inside."

When I am in grade 7, a fire starts in our basement, electrical we are told, smolders and erupts. My mom is one block away, shopping uptown in the IGA where our father works, my five-year-old brother with her. She hears the siren, turns toward the front of the store. "It's yours," someone yells, "your house is on fire." She grabs my brother, runs into the plate glass window, staggers back, shakes her head, runs out the door, down the hill to our house, her heart hammering.

Her muscles big as our dad's, our mom takes on the charred and stinking house. Raises a ball-peen hammer, smashes down the walls, lath and plaster and dust thick in the air. Hauls out 2 by 4's, 4 by 6's, gets up on the roof, shovels off the asbestos tiles, hauls them out back by herself. Crowbars the chicken coop along the fence, heaves the boards over. She helps dry-wall, grout, does all the painting. She cooks, makes our clothes, plays gymnastics with us, wrestles with our dad, tries to explain sex to us. My sister listens, I get up out of the bathtub, storm naked through the living room, past my brothers and dad watching hockey, yelling "no privacy, there's no privacy in this house."

She joins a ball team, a game that helped save her life when her mother died. First base or pitcher, her aim is fast, stinging. Almost every game she hits a homerun out of the park. My face burns when she tags someone out, throws to third, dead-on. Or stands, bat cocked at the plate or arm cocked on the pitcher's mound, steps into the play.

GRADE EIGHT. Spring. We are learning about earthworms, about the way they lie side-by-side to reproduce. We smell sap on the buds outside.

I don't remember whether the principal called Barry Kemper over the intercom or someone came to get him. He came back to class, his face red, two white circles on his cheeks. Barry's dad. The mine. His dad, small and quiet. He and the other fathers wait for the bus uptown in the early mornings or late evenings, a regular yellow school bus. Their faces are clean, their clothes washed, lunch buckets under their arms. After shift they get off the bus, shoulders slumped, feet heavy, their faces streaked with coal, even though they've all showered together in the washhouse.

Barry's dad trapped in the mine. Barry's dad and two others. In complete blackness. On a ledge.

The smell of buds outside, earthy smell of worms. In the hallways we whisper. "Did they find them yet? It's been three days, what the hell are they doing?"

EVERYDAY MY FATHER WORKS at the back of the IGA where he cuts meat, sings all day, his tenor voice sweet and strong up and down the aisles. "The singing butcher," people in the Crowsnest Pass call him, "he's our singing butcher." My mother encourages him and when I am in grade 10 he gets a band together, sings in the Miners' Club, the Legion, the Bellevue Inn.

"No kid of mine is ever going underground," he says, often, "I didn't go down and neither are you." He frowns at my two little brothers. This is years before he tells management in the IGA to fuck off because they want to make him meat manager and pay the women he works with less, catches a school bus every morning to the strip mine in BC, spends all day loading chemical blasts, running and ducking behind a digger shovel, tons of earth and coal blowing up into the air like atomic clouds. I will have moved away already, to the city, when he becomes a powder-man, but visit on weekends, smell the chemicals leaching from his pores.

In grade 12 we are told to take the permission form home for our parents' signatures if we want to spend the day down a working mine. That evening I forge his signature upstairs in the bedroom my sister and I share. A few boys and two other girls bring the form back signed.

We stand in the mine entrance, battery packs strapped onto our waists, lamps on our heads. A cold wind blows out of the darkness into our faces. The enormous metal fire-door bangs shut behind us. Complete darkness. Everything suddenly loud – my class-mates' breathing, swish of clothing, crunch of coal under boots, water dripping. I start to shiver. "Turn on your carbide lamps", the miner leading us says, "and don't get separated from the group."

Beams of light from our heads pierce the darkness. We turn to look at each other, blinding light, until we learn not to look in each others' faces. "Stick together," the miner says, turns and walks away, explaining about timbering tunnels, bolting the ceiling so it doesn't collapse, the dangers of pockets of gas.

I lag behind, wait until the others' pricks of light grow tiny in the dark. My own lamplight beams out over my eyes, lands feet in front of me on a black patch of undulating coal. I turn my head left and right and up and down. I can see only what my light falls on. A bit of black wall, a ceiling bolt, a puddle of water. Bits and pieces embedded in blackness. I look down at my hands, cannot see them until I raise them into the single beam of light. My feet, too, lost in the dark. Connected by darkness, separated by darkness. I run to catch up.

All day we trudge up hills, down dips, into freezing water, through tight crawl spaces.

"IF I'D WANTED TO MARRY A MAN, I would have," my father tells my mother in her ball uniform, glove over her shoulder. We all walk to the ballpark at the base of the mountain behind Bellevue. First base or pitching, she throws a mean left hook. She doesn't look at us in the packed stands. Her turn to bat. My stomach flutters. My father sighs. The back catcher from the other team squats, "put her here, big buddy," she sings to the pitcher, "easy batter, big buddy, easy batter." My mother stands with her bat cocked, stares at the pitcher. The pitcher draws her arm back, lifts her right foot, steps forward, lets go. The ball sings toward my mother. She steps toward the ball, swings the bat in slow motion. Crack, and the ball flies into the air, over first base, over left field, spins toward Turtle Mountain.

WHEN HE IS DYING OF LYMPHOMA, my father sits in a lawn chair in the backyard, staring up at the mountain where he once let his horse go wild. He has just turned 50. "That's where I want you to spread my ashes." He points, his arm shaking. "Up in that clearing there."

"LUNCH," THE MINER SAYS. He leads us around a bend. A group of men sit together, backs against coal, enough light between them that we can see their faces, their black-lined eyes. We all sit together, pull out our sandwiches, our hands and faces covered in coal-dirt. I bite into my sandwich, chew, coal-grit crunching between my teeth.

One of the men looks at me, careful to keep his light out of my eyes, "You're a girl. Jesus, there's a girl down here. Who's your family?"

At the end of the day, muscles aching, hardly able to lift our feet, we walk out into a cloudy day that hurts our eyes with its brightness. The other girls and I sit on the ground outside the wash-house while the men and boys shower. We ride home covered in coal.

The bus drops me off in front of my house above the Bellevue mine. My father's car is already there. He meets me at the backdoor, looks at my filthy face, my filthy clothing, frowns. The corners of his mouth twitch. "You'll just have to change out here in the yard."

EVERY SUMMER we hike up the old mine road, up the mountain above Bellevue. My sister and brothers, sisters-in-law, their children, my husband and I. We scramble up ridges, duck tree branches, climb small cliffs. The children are nimble and sure-footed.

We are sitting on top of a ridge, dangling our feet, holding the children's hands. The valley opens out below us. Across the valley the sun sits on top of Turtle Mountain.

"Look," I say, pointing to the rooftops in the valley below, "that's Bellevue, and there's Gramma's house."

"I miss Bellevue already," one of my nieces whispers, "whenever I look at Gramma's wrinkly elbows I fall in love. Now I'm in love with Bellevue."

Tea Leaves

A PLAY BY ROSALIND PRICE

CAST:

Celeste – just turned 6 years old. Looks like a troll.

Rosalind – her older sister, 9 almost 10 years old. Small and scrawny, with long wavy brown hair.

Clancy – a girl from Rosalind's class. Tall and scrawny, with fine red hair to her shoulders.

Rosalind's and Celeste's mother – 26 years old. A bit plump and muscular, with smooth caramel hair. Talks loud.

Clancy's mother – 35 years old. Tall and elegant, with red hair in a French roll.

ACT I

Rosalind and her sister Celeste are outside in their yard, banging rocks together to make a fine, stinky white powder that later Rosalind will mix with mud and bugs and make Celeste eat, Celeste's head tipped to one side, her face scrunched up so her cheeks stick out and she looks like her troll doll.

The gunshot sound of rocks slammed together ricochets off the boulders at the edge of the cliff, like when their dad sets up a target and lets Rosalind shoot the rifle by herself and the echo ricochets in her ribs and ears.

Celeste and Rosalind both look up at the same time and there, wandering the ditch toward them, head down, wind lifting her thin red hair, is the girl Clancy from Rosalind's class, tall and gangly and always trying to hide. Every few feet she hesitates, squats, reaches out and pets the rocks and boulders.

Celeste and Rosalind stop banging their rocks together, watch Clancy search the ditch toward them. When she's close enough for them to see the veins in her bone-skinny legs, she looks over at them, flinches.

Celeste: "You have funny –"

Rosalind clamps her dusty hand over Celeste's mouth, looks into Clancy's eyes – pale silvery-green as the Wolf Willow beside the river or the sage Celeste and Rosalind roll between their fingers and sniff – gone flat the way they do in school when the teacher talks to Clancy or one of the other kids turns to look at her at the back of the class where the teacher lets her stand to recite poetry. They all take turns reciting, but the teacher lets Clancy and Rosalind stand at the back, Clancy because she goes curdled white and faints if the other kids watch her, Rosalind because she grows hot and weak and cannot stop shaking and will run out the back door if any-one turns and looks at her.

Rosalind: "I am my father's son."

Rosalind watches Clancy's silvery-sage eyes to see if Clancy recognizes the line from the silent reading activity kit at school, the kit Rosalind and Clancy devour, story by story, coloured section by coloured section.

Clancy looks blank, and Rosalind's face begins to burn.

Then Clancy nods, her thin hair splitting over her shoulders.

Clancy: "Does your mother know?"

Rosalind looks blank. She thinks of her mother in the house with Alyd and her baby brother, Captain Huff and Puff, her mother's deep green eyes like the Crownsnest River, the way her mother can sew Rosalind and Celeste cowgirl outfits with fringes and fancy vests, and she always knows what to do if they burn themselves or get slivers or their necks swell up with mumps and they can't swallow.

Rosalind's and Celeste's mom sticks her head out the door, yells as loud as if they were down the cliff by the river.

Rosalind's and Celeste's Mother: "Rosalind. Celeste. Dinner."

Clancy watches Rosalind's mom over lunch scoop macaroni and tomatoes onto their plates with a bang, spoon mashed vegetables into Rosalind's baby brother's mouth, tell a story, her hands waving, eyes flashing.

Rosalind's and Celeste's Mother: "Their dad and me used to ride horses up these mountains. One time a sow black bear strode into our camp with two cubs, ate our whole God-damn supper. The buggers even drank our tea, ate our peaches real dainty and left the stones. As they were leaving, the sow stood up on her hind legs and the cubs tried to stand on their hind legs but kept falling over."

Rosalind's mom leaps out of her chair, acts out the mother bear on her hind legs, staggers around the kitchen like the baby bears.

Rosalind's and Celeste's Mother: "She couldn't get those little buggers out of there. She'd whoof for them to follow and walk off into the trees a bit, but they were too busy looking for food and dancing around on their hind legs. She kept coming back and swatting them. They'd fly ass over tea kettle, roll around on the ground bawling, but the next time she walked off what did they do? Got up on their hind legs and danced."

Rosalind's mom pretends she's the sow chasing her cubs and swatting them to try to get them out of camp.

Clancy laughs out loud, her silvery-sage eyes sparkling when Rosalind's mom falls to the floor, begins rolling and bawling like the cubs.

After lunch, they all go outside and Rosalind's mom elephant walks Rosalind and Celeste and Alyd around the yard, their legs clamped around her waist, their heads and arms hanging down, their hands clutching her legs.

Clancy stands off to one side, watching.

Rosalind's Mother: "Your turn. "

Clancy shakes her head no.

Rosalind's mom picks Rosalind up, flips her into the air. Turtle Mountain and the sky and the rocks somersault around Rosalind. She lands on her feet in the gravel.

Celeste runs toward their mom.

Celeste: "My turn, my turn."

Clancy looks away as Celeste flips through the air.

When Clancy's leaving, Rosalind's mom gives her a container of macaroni and tomatoes, rests her hand gently on Clancy's shoulder.

Rosalind's Mother: "Tell your mother thanks for letting you come play with Rosalind."

ACT II

After school, Clancy walks Rosalind home, across the field, past Fidenato's and DeCelia's big red store, through the winding streets at the edge of town, across the highway, along the dirt road in front of Rosalind's house. Their shadows waver over the rocks and clumps of grass beside them. They look at the ridge, the grass trees sky mountains, laugh, fall silent.

ACT III

Rosalind and Clancy sit outside in Rosalind's back-yard, amidst glacial gravel and hulking boulders.

Clancy brushes Rosalind's hair, long strokes down Rosalind's back to her waist, while Rosalind stares across the valley at Turtle Mountain and Celeste hangs upside down from the swingset. Then they stand up, run to the barn at the back of the yard, look around to make sure Rosalind's mother is not watching. Rosalind and Clancy climb onto the roof while Celeste ducks inside the barn. Clancy and Rosalind jump off the roof of the barn onto the rocky ground and whoever's knees swell first is the loser and has to sit still while Celeste rubs on horse liniment she found in the barn.

ACT IV

Rosalind and Clancy walk the other way – through town toward the other wild edge of Bellevue built up against the cliffs and forests, to Clancy's house shaped like a barn and painted bright purple, perched on a ridge. Clancy leads Rosalind around the back because there are no stairs connecting the front door to the ground.

Clancy's mother sits at a table covered in tea cups, turns and gives Rosalind a slow smile, her eyes the same silvery-sage as Clancy's, and Rosalind is instantly in love with her long neck, delicate nose, creamy skin, red hair pinned up in a French roll.

Clancy's mother pours Clancy and Rosalind tea into cups so thin light shines through, her movements slow and elegant.

Clancy's Mother: "Clancy tells me you like to read. She says you wrote a play for you girls to act in. She says she didn't feel shy in your play because she got to be somebody else."

Rosalind looks at Clancy, but Clancy is looking away.

Rosalind's face burns, though she doesn't feel like running out the door, she feels like drinking in Clancy's mom's perfume and her long, elegant fingers. She lifts the tea cup that trembles in her hands, rattles against the saucer, drinks strong black tea.

Clancy's mother pours Rosalind more tea, inclines her head toward Clancy.

Clancy's Mother: "Did Clancy tell you I like to read? At one time I thought I might become a writer, but that was a long time ago, before I had children."

Her mouth too dry to speak, Rosalind shakes her head no.

Clancy's mother picks up Rosalind's cup, reads Rosalind's tea leaves.

Clancy's Mother: "You were a seer, that's why you have fathomless eyes. You were burned at the stake because people thought you were a witch."

Her heart hammering, Rosalind looks over at Clancy staring at the side of her mother's face. Clancy's mother laughs, leans toward Rosalind, her breath sweet and dizzying.

Clancy's Mother: "But that won't happen in this life. In this life you will become a playwright."

Clancy's eyes have gone flat. Her mother twirls her finger through the leaves in Rosalind's cup.

Clancy's Mother: "Did Clancy tell you about the voices?"

A high buzzing in Rosalind's ears, as if she is halfway down the cliff behind her house and cannot think what to do with her feet. She shakes her head no.

Clancy's Mother: "They talk to me all the time. They are talking to me now, telling me to cut my children's throats, poison them, burn the house down. They are as real to me as you are, but right now they're whispering, so I can argue them down. When Clancy was born, they told me she was a kitten and I should drown her, but my mother was there and she stopped me, and then the voices went away for awhile and I could love Clancy. They came back, more voices with each child. Now I leave when they start giving me directions on how to kill my children. I go to the Legion and drink until they pass out. Someone drives me home, and she looks after me."

Her luminous eyes so sad Rosalind wants to kiss them, Clancy's mother looks over at Clancy whose eyes look dead.

Clancy's Mother: "I'm telling you this so you won't be afraid when I start arguing with someone you can't see or hear, if you're ever allowed to visit again."

Clancy's mother stretches her head back, exposes her long creamy neck, speaks toward the ceiling.

Clancy's Mother: "This is a small town. Your parents will hear about me soon enough. I would sooner they hear the whole story."

In slow motion Clancy's mother brings her head down, kisses Rosalind on the cheek, her breath warm in Rosalind's ear.

Clancy's Mother: "It would be best for all concerned if you did not put any of this in your next play."

Then she stands and heads for the door, her red head balanced on her bone-china neck, and they don't see her again, even after Clancy and Rosalind make grilled cheese and popcorn for Clancy's little brothers and sisters and they all play charades and the sun disappears into the forest and they all crawl onto beds piled with coats and sweaters instead of sheets and blankets and next to Rosalind Clancy smells like tea and toast.

THE END.

Ethel Mermaid

Listen, I have a story to tell you, a story about Ethel Mermaid. I should be telling my Language Arts class, but this is a true story, and in grade six it's essential to be believed. Not if it's not a true story, of course. I've already written one of those for my assignment, about how a girl in the 1800s flew from the top of Crowsnest Mountain to the top of Turtle Mountain at least ten miles away without once flapping her arms.

Now, the boys will believe this is not true, but at least they will believe. You may not believe my story, but then I won't know, so it doesn't really matter, does it? And face it, I have to live in this world, and I simply prefer not to have my world full of people who I know don't believe.

But I'm wandering, aren't I? I used to think wandering was bad, before we took about learning styles in Health class. I came out a definite abstract random.

On my last language assignment, Mr. Sandwich (no, I did not make that one up) wrote in the margins over and over, "off topic, off topic." I wrote very nicely in the margin under his comment, "I'm sorry, but I don't think you understand me. You must be sequential, probably concrete sequential. I am abstract random. Please see me if you have any questions." I put it on his desk two nights ago, and haven't heard anything since, even though I gave him my phone number.

When I told my mother she sat at the table pulling perm rods from her hair. She always gives herself perms, and me and Betty (this is not my sister's real name, of course, because this is a story and if I use my sister's real name, you and the boys may not believe me). Some people say Betty looks like a troll with a perm. Some say I do too, but in this story it's only Betty who looks like that. My mother said I was born bum first, and she guesses that's just the way I see the world, and what better way to see.

Now, you see, we are back to my mother, and that's who this story is about – my mother and Ethel Mermaid. After my mother fluffed up her hair with one of those fork things, she ran red lipstick over her mouth. "Kiss me quick." She puckered her lips at Betty, who truly looks like a troll with a perm. "Nothing makes me sick." We both laugh, though I must say, lately puckered lips remind me of worms, and my stomach does a little dance. But this story is old, at least a year.

"Do it, Mom, do it, do it." Betty and I danced around the kitchen linoleum over millions of red white blue and green worms.

"Do what?" She wiggled her ears, her perm sliding back and forth over her forehead.

"No, not that," though we laughed and danced the worms dizzy. "The light bulb, you know, the light bulb." Each time Betty jumped, her hair stood straight up, before it came down and joined her head.

"Ah, the light bulb." Mom stood, ran her hands down her sides, smoothed her sleeveless blouse, her green plaid skirt. She put one foot on her chair, pulled her other one up behind, real slow. Her hair brushed the light bulb. She looked down at us. "What about the light bulb?"

"You know." Betty giggled, though I doubt very much that trolls giggle, and flicked on the light.

My mother's hair a permed halo. She tipped back her head, held her mouth close to the bulb. Betty and I so quiet I could hear them, the people some archeologists from Calgary say lived here eight thousand years ago, not in our house, of course, but here on the edge of the cliff overlooking Crowsnest River. I hear them whispering. She puckers her big red lips, opens her mouth wide, sings into the bulb. "I saw the li-iight. I saw the li-i-ght." Slow and husky, making her lips tremble.

"Want to go to a rummage sale tomorrow?" she asks after. She sits with her elbows on the table, though we aren't allowed to, her eyes green as the Crowsnest River. "What do you want to be?" she asks. I say a horse. Betty says a billy goat gruff. "What do you want to be, Mom?" From the bedroom, mewling, and she stands to go change or nurse our latest baby. "Ethel Mer–," she says as she turns, so I miss the last part. She wiggles her plaid skirt, walks out of the room singing. "There's no business like show business, there's no business I know."

It takes me a minute to figure out what she means, probably due to my abstract randomness. Ethel Mer–, wiggle, wiggle. Ethel Mer–, wiggle.

Of course, Ethel Mermaid, who else, must be a terribly romantic mermaid in one of the movies with faces my mother walks uptown to see where all the women look like they're under water.

I know – I dangled a participle in that last sentence. We learned how not to in Grade Five, but I really think there are times when you mean what you dangle more than if you don't dangle them. Knowing makes it all right. I don't think this is true for sin, because something is a sin, whether you know it or not, before you get to do it. Obviously, participles don't dangle before you get to dangle them, unless words are sinful.

This is important to this story, you see, because for a person who lives in an agnostic home, (I know agnostics; we did them in Social Studies), I am severely religious. Come to think of it, so is my mother. Whenever I bring up God, she says, "I don't believe in God. How could he let children suffer so much? Look at those homeless kids in Calgary." My parents don't know it, but they must believe in God to say they don't believe. So they must mean something else when they say that, but I haven't figured out what.

Betty and I find a piece of cardboard out in the shed. "I'll draw her, you help me cut her out and colour her," I tell Betty. I start at the bottom – long, curvy fins, like the rainbow trout in the Crowsnest. Under my breath I tell God, "This is not an idol, this Mermaid is not for worship, God." God knows already, but sometimes knowing that God knows you know is as important as not knowing what you do know. I draw her bum curved out, as mermaids always sit on rocks and there are plenty in the Crowsnest. Last year, (come to think of it, Grade Five was a fruitful year for me) I won a camera for memorizing scripture. I chose the parts about Jesus' birth. These I could learn off by heart, for who couldn't get teary about a baby in a cowshed, if she was the oldest of five? And a pregnant woman on a donkey, I could feel that. When mom was pregnant with Emrys, she let us put our hands on her belly, and he tickled our palms.

I give her big breasts, who knows, maybe mermaids nurse, even Ethel. My hand shakes a bit; I keep seeing my mom's swollen-up blue veins and I feel so, I don't know, excited. Another girl memorized almost as much as me, she's new in Bellevue, her father drinks, but Reverend White handed me the camera. Then I got to thinking about Jesus telling his disciples to strip naked right there on the road and follow him, and he sure didn't say bring a camera. They left out too much anyway, in that story, didn't say once how Jesus smelled. A camera tells you how someone looks, but babies smell sweet and Jesus worked all day with wood. I'd sure like to know how he smelled. Most of all, I'd like to know what his mother thought or said. I told Reverend White that I'd made a mistake, I'd recited the same verses twice. Maybe he knew I was lying, but then again, maybe he didn't.

I give her big lips and permed hair. Betty starts cutting out her fins. I tried Baptist, but they kicked me out. After a sermon about God being all-knowing, all-seeing, infinite, I stood up and asked, "How could God possibly be a man?" Then I tried Dutch Reform. They even let me sing in the choir. I had to make up my own sermons, though, as I couldn't understand Dutch. Mine were usually about fist fights between Mary Magdalene and Satan in the desert, where Mary Magdalene wins, then comes back to town all sweaty, and Jesus runs up to her and she kisses him on the neck, and he smells like fresh cut wood. I told one of my friends in the choir. She must have told her parents, because the next thing you know, the Dutch Reform kicked me out.

"Get used to back doors," was all my mother said. "You think Jesus came in the temple through the front door?"

We spend all afternoon colouring her bright green fish-tail, red lips, yellow hair, green eyes, white breasts with blue veins, and very pink nipples. We hide her in the shed, slide her between two other cardboards. In bed we whisper about how we'll do it.

In the morning I say "I'm going uptown," grab some fishing line and a rod from the shed, running-shoe down the cliff to the river-bottom. I walk a long way upriver (there is no bridge near our house), cross over to the other bank, walk back downstream.

I never got beyond Ladies' Auxiliary Tea with the Anglicans. I came late. They were already eating little rolled sandwiches and drinking tea with their baby fingers in the air. So I did the same and listened to them talk about knotless embroidery. After awhile I thought we really should talk religion, so I waited for a quiet spot, then brought it up. "Look at us," I said, "a bunch of animals." I thought they were interested because they all stopped and looked at me. Nobody said anything, so I went on. "Just like God's other creatures, only we make choices." I really had their attention, then, so I continued. "Especially Reverend Harcourt," I said. "Under that black robe, he has the same parts as any other animal, even though he comes from England. Come to think of it, if Jesus could walk naked down a busy road, talking about fish and sheep, so can the queen of England."

Betty's troll head pushes out of the trees. I tie a rock onto my line, cast until it plops close to Betty on the other side. Betty wades in. Later, Mom will stick her hand in Betty's gumboot to see if we've been in the river. "Feeling is believing," she'll say. "You know you can't swim." I climb a Cottonwood, wedge the rod tight into a crook.

Back on the same side as Betty, I take the line I'd cast over, climb a tree, and tie the line around a thick branch. After the Anglicans kicked me out I tried the Catholic Church. In the catechism book Jesus always wears a sheet. So do his disciples. But he told them to strip naked. And the catechism book asks you questions that already have answers stuck in the back. And the women never get to say what they think. I wrote a letter to Father Denis, I didn't know him well enough to talk to him, about how we should put on a play in which Jesus strips naked and his disciples follow him, and at last, at last the women speak. I said if he was looking for someone to write it, I knew just the person.

"You did what?" My mother laughed until she peed. "After five babies my bladder ain't what it used to be."

After supper, Betty and I sneak out our bedroom window, grab *her* out of the shed, climb down the cliff. "Okay," I tell Betty. "Scream." Betty can scream like nobody's business. We both scream, loud as we can. "Mom, Mom, Mom."

We hear her feet crunch across the yard, "Jesus Christ, Jesus Christ, what the hell's going on?"

When I see her silhouette reach the edge, "Okay," I say to Betty, "turn it on."

In the beam of the flashlight, she rises up out of the water, Ethel Mermaid, bright green curves, white breasts, permed hair, thick lips, and I swear I hear her sing, I swear her lips tremble, all the way across the river into dark trees, *I see the li-i-ight, I see the light.*

The First Letter of Rosalind
to the Four Churches
of the Village Bellevue

GRACE, PEACE, AND MERCY TO YOU WHO kicked me out of your churches in the name of Jesus Christ, last year when I was eleven and obsessed with Jesus walking naked down the road telling his disciples to strip and follow and I could see their penises jiggle the way my little brother's jiggles when he runs naked down the back alley and my mom chases him, "Come back, you little bugger," but she's laughing and he thinks it's a game.

Pink, with a bit of blue under the skin when he's cold, but Jesus and his disciples were not cold in the desert. Except for night, of course, but I haven't thought of darkness or cold leaking up off the sand, up the hairs on Jesus' legs, making his skin bunch up and shrink and he puts his hands between his legs to stop shivering, the way my brother does when he gets out of Riverbottom Pond. He smells muddy before the sun bakes him dry, and a bit fishy. We wrap him in a towel, wrap our arms around him, rub his back and arms and the backs of his legs so the cold won't give him an asthma attack and he won't have to fall on his hands and knees at night, wheezing and shaking, his shoulders up to his ears, and his eyes when I turn on the light so far away, and we pray, even my parents who are severely agnostic, "Jesus, why should a little kid suffer," and he doesn't have enough air to cry. His penis so small when he runs out of the pond, like it wants to hide.

Where, I wonder, would Jesus hide when he shivers so hard his penis hurts, and does he ever wish he were a girl? Men had it tough in the Bible, and from watching you in church, I would say you have it tough too, standing around talking about Love, always turning your other cheeks, waiting to be smote by Angels of the Lord. "If they were women," my mom says, "they would know to damn well hug somebody and get warm."

"Cast off your sheets and your nets and follow me, boys," is what Jesus said. Having studied symbols and metaphors in grade six, I now realize that he might not have meant real sheets and nets. He might have meant abstract sheets and nets, the kind that are really ideas. When I told my mother about sheets not meaning sheets, but meaning something else that you can't touch, and nets meaning not the things we scoop trout out of the Crowsnest River with, but something bigger that you can't really fish with, that probably even the fish don't mean themselves but something we can't see, she said she was busy changing the ideas on the beds and how would we like to eat a big fat abstract fish for supper.

Now the reason I am writing this letter is to straighten out any misunderstandings you have about me and my religiousness. After all, Bellevue is a small town, and when I told my mom all four of you kicked me out, she said, "Watch it, you know what happened to Herod when he gave not God the glory."

You see, now that I'm in junior high school, I'm not so obsessed with the way Jesus smelled after a whole day of cutting and sanding wood, sweat prickling the soft insides of his arms, pooling in his bellybutton, or whether he ever got an erection in public or when he was alone at night lying on his back with the smell of cedar blowing in his window, and he closed his eyes and there was Mary Magdalene who knew how to hug people when she wanted to, smiling at him, her eyes green as my mothers, her lips big and soft, and who knows about her nipples or what they symbolize for him, though I wonder how you can possibly have the idea of a nipple without a nipple to get the idea from, even if you don't remember this was how you ate when you were a baby.

We learned about erections in the gym last spring when Dr. Hatfield came from Calgary and gave a talk on human anatomy and sexuality, with slides and a film. I wonder how Jesus felt lying on his back with his penis growing longer and harder, like when you stick your tongue out as hard as you can (this is a simile, I know, not a metaphor. I didn't say his penis is a tongue, but like a tongue. This is important.), only you can help sticking or not sticking your tongue out, but there is Jesus all alone with a father (not Joseph, of course, unless Joseph is like most of the fathers I know) he can't see or who never hugs him, his mother in the other room the way women are always in the other room in the Bible, probably making real food that Jesus eats for breakfast, maybe a fried trout or two, on his back in the dark with cedar blowing in his window, Mary Magdalene in his head smiling at him, and he doesn't know why but his penis grows hard, nuzzles his sheet and he breathes faster, because even you must admit, Brother Siddon, and you, Father Denis, that Jesus was a man even if he was a symbol and even if his penis is the idea of a penis, it behaves like any man's.

But, you see, I am not obsessed any more with Jesus' penis. I now realize that a penis is not important. Penis is just a word that stands for something else. Miss Murray told us this in English 7, only she said "rose." "A rose stands for the concept of love, or beauty, that's why we give roses on birthdays or anniversaries." But the only time my dad gave my mom a rose was just before he ran off with Darl Seebert. So I'm not sure yet what a penis stands for. I would be interested to hear what you have to say. You could write to me, General Delivery.

Concepts are what I am interested in now, the idea of being "eaten of worms," and what those words symbolize, and what it means he "gave up the ghost." I know they mean Herod in the Bible, but I am not interested in Herod. You once said, Reverend Harcourt, that many of the stories in the Bible are symbolic, and you, Minister van Delft, said they are all true. Well, I have this idea, you see, that the worms Herod is eaten of really represent his penis, or the ideas he has because he has a penis. They can't be real worms because real worms don't eat people when they are still alive.

Now, if Herod is eaten of worms because he has a penis, so are the four of you, and all of the men in your churches. So was my dad, which is why he gave up the ghost of our family and ran off with Darl Seebert. As for Jesus, he's eaten of worms because he can't give up the ghost, the Holy Ghost, because he is supposed to save the whole world, even people who don't want to be saved.

When I hold my little brother in his towel or at night on the edge of his bed and his body trembles every time he tries to take a breath or let one out, I pray that he won't be eaten of worms. I don't think he will be because people pay for their sins in the Bible, and my brother has paid in advance.

So, you see, I am interested in the idea of Jesus lying on his back with Mary Magdalene in his head and whether he touches his penis the way my little brother sometimes does and wonders, why him? This is when Mary Magdalene, the real Mary Magdalene outside Jesus' head, with her green eyes like my mother's, like the grass in the Crowsnest River, with speckles like the ones on a rainbow trout, deep and brown and you can see them swim through the grass and you know they can feel the grass caress their sides, wraps him in her towel, hugs him to her chest, tucks his shoulders under her armpits slightly sweaty, kisses his wet wet hair and whispers "It's okay, you'll be okay."

If a Mote

DUST MOTES WILD IN THE SUNBEAM SLANTING in the window. The window with Turtle Mountain framed, Turtle Mountain's grey missing face, scooped and gouged and dizzy. If the mote in thy eye offend thee, cast it out. But so many – flickering, sparking.

The people in their beds at the base of the mountain, April 1903, 3 or 4 or 4:30 in the morning, what did they see when the mountain fell? 90 million tons of rock? An enormous black shadow or a winged shade in the corner of the eye? An angel perhaps, a mote or moment of angel?

APPARENTLY BILLY BISHOP, WWI flying ace, had extraordinary long vision. So did Burling, WWII. According to Billy Bishop's son, Bishop and Burling were "fighters to the core." They trained their eyes to see specks on the horizon by looking at an object, looking away, then looking again. Focus, un-focus, re-focus.

"What is that, over there above those oak trees?"

"Nothing. I don't see a thing."

"Look again."

"Can't see a thing. Well, maybe a speck, maybe a crow."

"Wrong. A German bi-plane. Red nose. Flying at 7,000. We have five minutes."

MY COUSIN ASKED the surgeon before she went under to have the cancer removed, the cancer eating her breast, the lump that showed up in the bath and two weeks later was eating up into her shoulder, "What are my chances?"

"I can't say."

"Come on, don't bullshit me."

"We don't like to say."

"What are my chances of surviving six weeks? Fifty percent, sixty?"

"Five."

SEE THIS PICTURE? Black and white holds up better than colour. Ever notice in old colour shots how people turn pale green, fade away? Doesn't happen with black and white.

That little girl in the bathing suit, shoulders back, chin out, is my cousin. The woman behind her is my aunt. The man next to my aunt is my uncle. This is a child's way of seeing relations, "my" aunt, "my" uncle. The adult me would say "the woman behind my cousin is her mother, the man beside the woman is her husband," or "the man and woman behind my cousin are her parents," or "the man beside the woman is her husband, the girl in front is her daughter." And so on. The extended family I can name from various perspectives but hardly ever see, now that we are decades older and live in the same city.

The man on the other side of Auntie, doesn't he look young, hair slicked back, so young to be a father, my father, is her baby brother.

QUICKENING IS WHAT? A flutter, I'm told, deep inside the first time a fetus moves. How everyone in my family trades stories about what children say and how and the possibilities. My brother Al phones when Mikaila is two, "Hey, I was showing Mik countries on the globe, and when I showed her Algeria, she said, 'it's My Geria too.'"

"He wanted me to lie down with him for a nap," my aunt says about her great-grandson when he was four, "and I said, 'well you better not talk then.' You know what he said? 'Whatever you say, darling,' then fell asleep. Fast asleep, just like that."

"I don't know if that's what's causing the infertility," the surgeon says in the recovery room. She rests her hand on my leg. "It's possible that if you and your husband had married other people, you would have had children. You never know."

ONE WEEK ONE SUMMER I hiked the West Coast Trail with people I just met. One of the women grew up on the Island and knew how to read tide tables. When the tide was out we hiked along the beach, our bodies bent beautiful between clear sky and round rocks slippery brown and green.

We watched our feet dance over and between rocks and driftwood and whooshing blowholes that could wash us out to sea, crash our bodies against boulders. We watched our feet balance body and sky and pack and the possibility that we could, we could fall.

We scrutinized the cliffs on our right for climbable spots, in case the tide turned and surprised us squatting beside a tidal pool stroking a purple starfish, standing at the edge of the ocean mesmerized by sudden plumes bursting on the horizon, sudden glint and roll of killer whales.

In the afternoons we pitched our tents beside freshwater rivers running into the ocean. Not too close, in case of rain, in case the river swelled and lifted us unseeing in our tents and washed us out to sea. We rode logs down the river, fell off in salty spray, swam in deep freshwater pools. After dark we ate and talked and sang.

In the dark in my sleeping bag I dreamed I was trapped by slimy tree roots, in the dark and damp and sweating and twisted. In the morning I squatted on the beach, the ocean hissing and sighing at my toes, held my bowl in saltwater. The woman who could read tides came and squatted beside me. "Is there something wrong?"

I traced water droplets along my blue plastic bowl, "My father is dying."

"Is he sick?"

"Yes, but he doesn't know yet."

"How do you know?"

"I just know. Please hold me."

THAT LITTLE GIRL IN THE PHOTO, shoulders back, chest out, saucy grin, she's my cousin. Eight and everything she can't see ahead of her. High school and periods and pale pink lipstick and backcombed flips and three boy husbands she supports and chemotherapy and –

That girl on the right, she's my mom. The laughing baby in her arms, that's me. I am laughing at my uncle with the crooked neck holding the camera. "Fish, everybody say fish." I am laughing because my mom's hand around my chest tickles and she smells like milk and my dad beside us has black shiny hair and my aunt sings when she holds me, my ear on her chest, and my uncle beside her blows bubbles and my cousin scrunches up her face, bounces me around our tiny livingroom, feeds me chocolate, holds me asleep and none of us see what's coming.

MY BROTHER DID. Saw the car career into their lane. Lifted his feet onto the dash, braced himself. Saw it even as he was accepting a ride home from school with his friend, the careful driver in his red truck outside the school bus. "No, not today. Don't take a ride home today," my brother thought, even as he turned around and stepped out of the bus, climbed into his friend's truck, just as another friend climbed into the midnight-blue Dodge coupe revving beside them. "No," my brother thought, "don't ride with him."

ALL THE WAY HOME from the West Coast, images of my father's face trapped in slimy tree roots, the rising tide filling his mouth. My friend and I took turns driving. I drove from Creston to the Crowsnest, the steering-wheel solid, responsive under my fingers. In Fernie I thought about driving up to the ski hill, picking wild raspberries in the sun, but I needed to get home to the Crownsnest, lift my father's head from the sea foam drowning his lips, his eyes. My heart wouldn't stop hammering, my tongue stuck to the hard palette behind my teeth. East, past Sparwood, past the old tipple where Michel and Natal used to sprawl coal-grimy, around the Crowsnest Lakes where people say a train loaded with coins or liquor rests in the murk of the bottomless bottom, past the sulphur plant, through Coleman, past the high school, past the red brick hospital, through Blairmore, through the Frank Slide, sun on the limestone boulders, limestone boulders falling through the dawn, dust or motes or angels falling in our eyes.

I AM THREE and in a café in Calgary with my mummy and daddy waiting for chips and gravy waiting for my cousin, we live here now, my mummy and daddy and me, standing on my chair waiting for my cousin to walk in the door, daddy drove from Vancouver with his brother but the car exploded he smelled smoke "what the hell" they got out kaboom everything burned all our pictures, when is she coming hurry hurry, on the train how we came my mummy and me through the mountains click click hum hum look look how tall how steep, every time the door opens and the wrong people come in, when is she coming I need to see her we live here now come see our apartment in that red brick place the penguin by the service station come now oh hurry hurry, sun and sparkles every time the door opens, do you see her do you see her yet, walking in head back grinning, yes here here, up and down on my chair, here here, calling her name I can't say right sounds like "toilet" jump jump "oh toilet my toilet" her face red looking at me she starts crying turns and runs.

"I'M PREGNANT. I didn't know I was and the camel bucked me off and I'm so sick I can't stop puking." My sister's voice small and weak and far far away over the phone. The hollow emptiness in my abdomen quivering, I picture her on the camel's domed hump, Darwin Australia, numbing heat and monsoons and fresh mangoes dropping in the field across from her house and the camel snakes his head, leaps into the air, all four legs splayed straight out, spins. My sister's head snaps forward, back, she is flying, the crunch, the sick dizziness, looking around, crying. "Where's my mother, get my mother."

MY BROTHER AND HIS FRIEND in the pick-up truck drive past the hospital, along the main street of Blairmore, past Goat Mountain, through the village of Frank, into the Slide. Pale grey boulders. His friend drives the speed limit. "I could've taken the bus," my brother says to him, "you didn't have to come all the way to Bellevue." Miles of boulders on both sides of the highway, Turtle Mountain grey and faceless. A long straight stretch. My brother stares down the road, Bellevue around the corner ahead, looks up at the top of Turtle, looks back at the road, at the midnight-blue car careering into their lane, "Jesus Christ, what were they doing in Bellevue," lifts his feet onto the dash.

"TWO. THERE ARE TWO IN THERE." My sister's voice tongue-thick. "I can't eat or drink, can't keep anything down. I've been in the hospital for a week on IV. I'm scared. I didn't know I was pregnant. I'm so afraid they got damaged when I got bucked off. I can't stop crying. I'm going to have two babies at once and I keep thinking of you and I can't stop crying."

"What would you say," my brother asks over the phone, "if I told you we're expecting a baby and it was an accident and we're scared as hell and don't know how to tell you?"

"I hurt," I tell my mom on the phone, "I hurt and I'm jealous and I feel guilty."

Neighbourhood children come to climb my apple tree, eyes serious when I let them probe my ear lobes with an earring until the stem finally finds the hole and we all cheer and eat oranges outside in the sun while the girl who is 9 twirls her hair in tight knots against her scalp and tells about her mother's epilepsy and her father's illness and how they keep getting cut off social assistance and for lunches she and her little brother take slices of bread, no fruit or milk or cheese in the house, until bald patches cover the back of her head and I hire her and her little brother to help me wash out my car.

After they leave I curl around the buckling cramp in my uterus and cry and curse.

AMONG PALM TREES in the university solarium, statues of Plato and Aristotle and Socrates and the air moist with fetid earth and coffee and my friend's eyes behind her glasses moist and sad, twice she had attempted suicide, not cries for help but because she meant it. I leaned forward over the low table between us, plant damp and screech of metal chair legs against cement, the fan blowing fresh air into the palm leaves whined and cut in and out, in and out. I told her she was smart, funny, warm, talented, would she tell me if she felt suicidal again. For a while I believed in this garden, her eyes bright with novels she loved and a new boyfriend and hiking and cross-country skiing, until she stopped coming, long silences over the phone, missing her through the late winter snow lashing the solarium where I sat and waited, until a mutual friend told me what no one wanted to tell me, our friend had driven across the country to Newfoundland in the spring. Hikers found her body at the base of a cliff beside the ocean.

DUST IN THEIR EYES. Limestone dust and smoke rising from the valley as the miners step out of the air-shaft trembling, two dark days of digging and sweating and praying and cursing and imagining their families, milky kiss of their babies, bony knees and elbows of their children's running limbs, the bread and lavender smell of the hollows in their wives' throats. Imagining the coal around their friends' eyes in the town below where they lift mugs of beer. Two days smashing their picks into solid boulders in the dark, walls of rock between them and the entranceway, so they dig up toward the air-shaft. Rock between them and air, them and water, them and their loved ones asleep in their beds in the valley below. Two days of sweat and laboured breathing and wrestling, the fear warning them not to close their eyes, not to go to sleep. At last a prick of light wavers to them through the dark. "A cave-in," they will tell their friends and families when they themselves are safe in the valley, then they will tell how they dug and rested and hoped and despaired. The stories form in their heads as they dig toward the light, their bodies already ahead of them, already climbing out the air-shaft, drinking in light and air and the river and the town spread out below them. It takes a moment, dust in their eyes, for them to catch up with their bodies and the vision of miles of rock spread smoking and stinking over the valley below, register the percussion beneath their rib cages, fall onto their knees.

ELEVEN, MY MOTHER JESSIE, and she knew her mother was going to die. No one told her. Her mother had been rushed to hospital many times before, blue around her lips, eyelids sunk, wheezing gasping. On the farm where they took her and her brother, "Your mother's sick, she needs a rest," the man collected snakes. Stuck a needle dipped in iodine through their temples. Eleven and on the farm one morning, weeks before her mother's heart exploded, six years before she had me, my mother woke up with a dying snake coiled around her throat.

IN CALGARY my cousin used to take the bus to our house, take me by the hand to the outdoor swimming pool. A big kidney-shaped pool, painted white. We stripped down to our bathing suits on the mounded grass, waded in. Warm and cool on my shins, knees, thighs. Bright glinty suns slipped, slid, leapt over the water. "Lay down," my cousin said, "lay down, I'll hold you." Her hands under my arms holding me stretched out in the water, lapping up over my shoulders. "Hold your breath and put your face in." Her voice behind my head. "See if you can keep your eyes open, like they taught me at swimming lessons." I take a deep breath, dunk my face, cold and sun lines slicing through water, oh my eyes, arch my head back sputtering. "Good," she says, "good, now hold your arms out in front of you like this and just lay down. I'll hold you." On my knees, arms over my head, her hands tight around my waist, I lean into water, cold up over my face, my ears, my hair swirling, arms head legs, waist stretched flat. Where are her hands, where did she? My head sinks bum rises, where, where are you? Her hands hoist me by my arms, my hair plastered to my face. "You'll never learn to swim," she says, shaking her head. "Your head is too heavy. That happens for some people. Their heads are just too heavy."

All afternoon I walk my hands along the bottom of the white painted pool, swim my body through water warm and cool, dunk my face up to my ears and watch my fingers wave. My cousin swims back and forth, her arms arching over her head, her face in and out of water. After we eat our peanut butter sandwiches, she holds a towel up so I can peel my wet suit down my tummy, my legs. "Don't worry," she says, "I won't let anyone see you naked."

I RAN AHEAD of my friend into the house. My father sat at the kitchen table, eyes half-closed. His skin yellow, lips white. "Dad?" I touched his shoulder, "Dad?"

"So tired," he whispered, "so goddamned tired. Tried to mow the lawn, but I can't, can't." He opened his eyes, looked up at me. His drowning eyes.

"Dad listens to you. You see if you can get him to go see Dr. Utley." My mom's eyes jiggle back and forth. Green. Green as the grass in the Crowsnest River. Speckled. In all my writing, my mother's eyes and river grass and speckled trout flit flitting. Dr. Utley shakes her head, "I'm not sure, but I think it's leukemia. I'm sending him by ambulance to Calgary."

MY BROTHER WATCHES the midnight-blue coupe career into their lane. Pushes his feet into the dash. Shit, this is it. Shit. The next thing he remembers is clambering over the rocks above the highway, looking down on the accordioned truck, the severed car. No one else around, he hears a voice, "Look at that. Alyd Price was in an accident." A red car pulls off the highway between the accordioned truck and car. "Alyd Price. An accident." A siren screams through limestone boulders. "Alyd Alyd Alyd. Price Price Price." The policeman ushers him and his friend into the back of the ambulance, sits them down beside the boy who shouldn't have taken a ride in the Dodge coupe, stretched out on the ambulance bed, covered to his chin in a white blanket, his eye bruised and bloody, hanging out of its socket. He moans. A siren screams. Owowowowowowowowow.

THIS IS THE FIRST GRIZZLY BEAR DREAM. My cousin and I are playing in a meadow. She is walking on her hands, her face flushed red. I laugh and spin, my arms stretched out. And there it is. A bear. Ambling out of some poplars into the meadow. It stops, sniffs the wind, shakes its head side to side. "Run," I yell at my cousin, "run." She vaults onto her feet. We stand still and stare at the bear, big and blonde in the sun, staring at us. The air quivers. My legs shake but we stand still. The bear stands still. Wind ruffles the hump behind its head. Suddenly it stiffens. Whoofs. And we are running. Our feet pound, my heart pounds, my arms churn. My cousin passes me. Behind, the grizzly's whoofing breath. Ahead, a tall Cottonwood. My cousin gets there first, shimmies to the lowest branch, scrambles for the next. My chest burns, my legs pump. "Please please please," I whimper. The bear's breath hot on the back of my neck. Whoof and it lunges past me, hooks my cousin's calf, pulls her out of the tree, rolls her along the ground.

"MIKAILA LOOKS LIKE YOU," my brother says on the phone. "Even Mom thinks so." All the way to the hospital I clench and unclench my fists. Inside the door of the Intensive Care Unit I pull on a gown and gloves. My arms heavy, back stiff, I grit my teeth. Push through the double doors. And there she is, naked in a plastic box, tubes up her nose, one side of her head shaved and I'm not angry but something else I don't know, she's alone in a plastic box, breath of tubes up her nose, looking out, her first view of the world.

"Angry," says the nurse. "Went red with rage when we pricked her heel for blood." I lean my head against the wall, oh Mikaila Mikaila.

IN THE CROWSNEST. Where we move in the last months of grade four. In the house we rent on the edge of the cliff. Wood-and-coal stove my mother fries the steaks on because my father is the butcher in town, stands at the back of the store whistling and singing, brings steaks home when they turn brown and no one wants them, insists on paying full price. Whistling and singing, his black hair slicked back, my mother's hair tawny in the sun of our yard. Glint of coal in the wild grass next to the field on the edge of the cliff. Steak sizzling in a cast-iron pan. My mother hooks it with a fork, flips it over, my brother and sister and father and me and even Gareth, our sweet one-and-a-half-year-old baby, we all call him "our" baby, stand around the stove, "God, that smells good," linoleum cold under our feet. Around the table we lean over our plates, "Look, so tender you can cut it with a fork." Steak juicy in our mouths.

Can't sleep in the tiny room I share with my sister and brother, spiders down there in the dark under the covers around my ankles, pull my knees up to my chin, shiver on top of the blanket. "Black widows," I read in Calgary in school, in the dark, "highly venomous." My teeth chatter, knees shake. The covers underneath my hip, cold, long night stretching ahead, forever, tiny sharp bites of spiders, shivering.

"Go to sleep," Mom whispers from the next room.

"I can't, there's a spider in my bed."

"Don't be silly, you're imagining it."

"No, Mom, it's here, I can tell."

"Please, just get under the covers and go to sleep."

"Mom, I can't, don't you know about black widows?"

"There are no black widows here, now just crawl in and go to sleep."

"No."

"Look, if I have to come in there and make you sleep under the covers you're in trouble. Do you hear me?"

Paralysis of spider venom, sharp prick in the ankle, electric current up my legs, up into the back of my throat, can't swallow, can't move. Her bare feet crossing the room, flash of the light and her hands pulling the covers out from under me, throwing them back and three spiders – a daddy-long-legs, a tiny white, tiny black – curled where my feet should have been.

APRIL 29, 1903. Early hours of the morning, last flicker of darkness. What dreams, the people in their beds in the village of Frank? What inhalations, tastes on the tongue, twitching muscles? Shudder, groan, and ninety million tons of rock let loose. Ninety million tons. Groan and shudder and flutter or burst of eyelids, muscles, boulders, wind in their beds, at their doors. In bedclothes, in flight, not knowing where, or why. That mote that moment that angel that.

MY MOTHER PHONES ME. "Your brother's been in an accident." I sit naked on the end of my bed. "Head-on. He's fine, the other boy is fine, but the two in the other vehicle are dead. He's in shock, but he wants to talk to you."

My brother, so far away over the phone, my brother crying, "I don't know why he accepted a ride home, now he's dead, his eye, his eye, why did he, they pulled the curtain, if he hadn't, into our lane, why were they, just one second later."

My brother when he was a baby, his blonde baby hair, round eyes rolled up, shaking twitching and the doctor, "You won't have him long."

SEE THIS PHOTO? It was taken at our wedding reception, in our living room. Notice how my dad and his sister and his niece look as if they've just landed, as if they can't stay long? Everyone else looks solid, don't you think? My friend sitting on the arm of the couch. My sister leaning against the wall. My mother, her hand bringing food to her mouth. Their dresses, pink and blue and green, their faces flushed, feet on the floor. But Dad and Auntie and my cousin, blur of their faces, their bodies.

"DO YOU WANT ME TO COME OVER and look after you," she asks on the phone and here we are dancing around the living room, Mikaila and I, k.d. lang's "big-boned gal from Alberta" in our muscles, lift our shoulder knees arms, spin and swirl. Sun coming in the window dancing along Mik's naked two-year-old skin, that far-away look in her eyes when music's in her muscles.

"You look a lot like me today, Roz."

"Do you think so, Mik?"

"Yes, you do, you look just like me."

"Why is that, do you suppose?"

"Because I came from your tummy, your tummy and mommy's."

"Well, actually, Mik you can only come from one woman's tummy, and you came from your mummy's."

"No, Roz, I came from your tummy, too. I know."

MY MOTHER TELLS ME she literally died of an asthma attack once. In the hospital. She was already there because of asthma. This was when we lived in New Westminster where I was born. She was eighteen. I was ten months old. Alone in her room gasping for air, heart fluttering, chest burning. Spasm in her chest and her heart. Stopped. Her mother dressed in white on top of a hill, beckoning, "Come on, Jessie, you can make it, you can make it." Her mother she hadn't seen since she was eleven, her mother not dead, not brittle and frail and black around the eyes. Her mother plump and smiling, waving, "Come on, Jessie, you can make it." And she would have, except for the intern on her chest, thumping her ribs, "Come on, come on, you can make it."

MOMENTARY IS THE WORD I was looking for. That moment of being. Moment of recognition. And resonance. "If I would have known years ago how sick she'd be now, I wouldn't have had her." My aunt shakes her head, my aunt after forty-two weeks of chemotherapy for bowel cancer, her eyes behind her glasses large and brown. "No, I wouldn't have."

I KNOW A WRITER who wrote a book about her father's death. A poignant book. A slow death. At a retreat in the Crowsnest Pass, surrounded by rocks and lakes and stories of mine disasters, falling mountains, shoot-outs, "Too much tragedy," she says as we ride in a van through the Frank Slide, boulders strewn across the valley, "there is too much tragedy." Later someone tells me that this writer's mother is dying of the same illness her father died of. In the evening, before she reads in this place that used to be a hospital and nursing home, where just through those doors and up those stairs my father rolled over, sighed, slipped away from his ravaged body, the writer stands in front of the fireplace, "Before, I used to write about tragedy, but now that there is so much tragedy in my life, I don't want to write about it."

MY BROTHER AL holds Mikaila against his chest. Her tears on his neck. He strokes the back of her head. "What's wrong, Mik?"

"I miss him so much."

"Who do you miss, Mik?"

"My granddad I never met. He went to bed and died and now I'll never get to see him."

A FEW MONTHS AFTER her mother died, my mother was walking along 8th Ave. downtown Calgary. Snow blew in her face, swirled around her ankles. Past Agnew Shoes, the Café where she would waitress in two years, the bakery with hard-iced cakes in the window. At the corner of 8th and 1st she stopped to wait for the walk light, squinted through the snow at the Bay across the street. Grey stone columns and arches and just coming around the corner, tiny in her brown coat, shoulders back, oh please, please, yes, yes, wait. "Wait for me, mom. Wait for me." Ran through the cars the buses, "Mom. Mom." Ran up to the woman, threw herself against her chest, wrapped her arms around her waist. "Mom. Don't leave, please don't leave."

The woman held her, stroked her hair, "I wish I could be your mother. I wish this moment I was her."

"WELL, I'M NOT DEAD YET, am I?" My cousin's hand stroking the cheek of one of her small nephews. "And my hair's growing back. What more could I want?" She laughs, sighs. "I'll just have to wait and see."

SHE PHONES ME BY HERSELF. "Hey Roz, I want to talk to you about trees and rabbits. What kind of trees were on your hike?"

"Fir trees and pine trees, Mik."

"Did you see palm trees?"

"No, no palm trees."

"Did you see any rabbits?"

"No, no rabbits. We were making too much noise."

"How about beavers, beavers diving like dolphins?"

"No, no beavers either. But we saw a waterfall coming out of a mountain."

"Wait, I'm getting a pen and paper to draw it. Was the mountain a triangle?"

"Kind of."

"Like this?"

I close my eyes, picture her holding her drawing up to the phone. "Yes, kind of like that."

"How high was the waterfall?"

"Oh, about a hundred feet."

"Yup, I drew it a hundred feet. Now, let's be magic. Can you see?"

Hoar Frost

PLAIN PROSE, TODAY I WANT TO WRITE PLAIN prose. I want to write, "Yesterday the sun didn't come up & hoar frost clung to the trees." I read the newspaper, *Teenage Girl Lived in Fear, Stabbed to Death by Boyfriend*. I want to write comfort, not sorrow. I want to write hot milk in the belly. The belly of my arm lying beside the headline, *Women Struggle to End Violence Against Women*. Trees wearing hoar frost, white & heavy. Trees wearing hoar frost in the fog. *Woman Murdered by Ex-Husband, Neighbours Say She Was a Wonderful Person*. I want to write plain prose about the surprise of trees coming out of the fog wearing hoar frost all day. On CBC Radio a male announcer's voice, "Tomorrow's question on Cross-Country Check-Up — now that we have a female astronaut in space, has feminism outlived its purpose?" Plain accessible prose. I want to make it plain.

OW CHUT, WRITES MY FRIEND. Seed growing. Seeds growing. Into trees wearing hoar frost, surprised out of the fog. Plain prose of seeds growing, starting with "plain prose, today want to write." So many seeds. The boyfriend saying, "I'd sooner kill her than see her with someone else." Four people he tells & they walk around with this seed, thinking who knows what, maybe hoping, but not telling, not arranging protection. Prosaic as the words "protection" or "political will." And the girl, fear sending roots down into her intestines, hard branches up her lungs, carries a knife just in case. Or "seed of doubt," we say, "is there a seed of doubt?" But wanting to write plain prose about the trees heavy & beautiful & surprising out of the fog, not the pain eating up my back & neck & shoulders. Plain as 1:50 when a friend phones, "I'm coming to you." Accessible as five orange oranges with green leaves & stems, sticky bean rice cake, red tin of Oolong Tea, sesame bean balls she pulls out of her pack. "I'm thinking about writing," I say, "I'm thinking about not writing."

ORANGES, I WANT TO WRITE. Not the blade of a knife. Oranges. Sweet and seedy-segmented. Orange seeds on my tongue. How often I write "tongue." How my friend and husband and I go together to her sister's house. Hoar frost on the trees, trees coming out of the fog, we are laughing, oranges on our breaths, on our fingers. Fog on the river, hoar-frost on the trees. "Come in," she says, "come say hello to my sister and brother-in-law and nieces and nephew from Vietnam." Into the kitchen. A pot of boiling broth, rice wraps, noodles, squid, beef slices, lettuce, cucumber, & coriander & mint & beer. "Happy New Year, Happy Vietnamese New Year, one week early." Into clink of glasses. Into talk of knives. Knives my friend's brother-in-law carried when he went to tell the farmers what crops & how, knives because he worked for the government, knives even though friends. A degree in horticulture, & knives. "Two jobs," he says, "I must work two jobs here. Maybe when my kids grow up I can go back to school." Two jobs, my friend's sister works two jobs seven days a week. A rice wrap, lettuce, cucumber, noodles, squid, mint, & roll it up. Roll. Happy New Year. Plain as generosity, aromatic as oranges.

Today I want to. Plain prose about the coffee pot on the table, half-full, and the choice of words. Luxury like coffee. Choice of "I want" or "half-full" or "today." Focus on the coffee. Bean. Being. Grounds. Floating half-way. The newspaper beside my cup. *Woman Abducted from Store in Small Town, Feared Dead.* The lightness of coffee ground in a machine in a shop, floating on the surface. *Family Waits in Fear as Police Search for Missing Woman.* Weight of the plunger pushing the grounds to the bottom of the pot. Ground into, or on the. *Body Found in Field.* Predictability of the grounds sinking, coffee bubbling up. "Things like this just don't happen in small towns," says a resident. "Women here haven't had to fear the way they do in cities. Now we all have to fear." The way coffee smells better than it tastes. "I thought he was joking," says a neighbour. "You know how some guys like to brag. I never thought he actually killed someone. He was a quiet kinda guy." Plain as the grit at the bottom of the cup, grit in my teeth.

HOW I WANT TO WRITE "seeds spun from the Poplar tree, spun down and around, landed in the new snow." Or hoar frost on the crab apples outside my window. "Heavy and hoary." Plain as that, as the ache in my tongue, behind my teeth when I think "frost" and "apples." Plain as the lit street where a man attacked my friend, knocked her down, kicked her head, broke her nose. Plain as "I just can't read or write or think about that stuff" or "help me, please somebody help." Plain as the woman stopped on her way home from work, shot twice in the head, buried in a field. Or my mother when she was eleven, dragged out of town beside the river, beaten and raped. The sound, the impact of boots and bullets when we are inside or out of our heads. With fear, we say, "I was out of my head with fear." Or not. Plain as that. Where we sit over coffee, my friends and I, lift foamy milk to our lips, laugh at the warmth on our tongues, our teeth, in our bellies. And coffee, not because it's coffee, but just because.

ACCESSIBLE AS THE COFFEE POT on the table or
"Would you like a cup of coffee?" Common as
"hello." Prose plain as the period at the end of a sentence, the comma in the middle. Today I want to
write plain plain prose. Except for the coffee beans
and where they come from and how we rarely talk
with people who have no choice but to burn their
forests for coffee trees and even then can they make
enough to live on. Today I want to focus on the coffee pot. On the beans. Already sliding into "being."
And ground. The grounds at the bottom of the pot,
the ground under the soldier's boot on the front page
of the newspaper. A Rwandan soldier lifting the
corpse of a child. A girl. Her arms up stiff. I want to
write about hiking through cow parsnip and
magenta paintbrushes and wild strawberries, up the
trail between rocky cliffs, to the lake nestled among
the peaks. "Nestled," I want to write "nestled." Or
"Here at the lake a gold-eye duck swims with her
three chicks, and the chicks are fluffy and downy and
climb onto their mother's back." But the child on the
front page. A girl. Children fall down. But down,
grounded. A soldier helping her up, but she is dead.
Three downy chicks behind the rock in the middle
of the lake. Water, millions of children men women
without water. How the yellow flowers keep living
on the bottom of the lake. And you can't bring her
back. Bring her up, arms stiff, head hanging. Coffee
pot lake child dead politicians women soldiers guns
run ribs tongue stuck to stuck to. Mud so clear
through the water, all the water.

SURPRISED OUT OF THE FOG. Into sun on the Cottonwood trees. Sun up the bark into the branches. Gold and glowing. Looking for birds. A flick, hop, bounce, flit. Looking. *Suburban sprawl and river pollution may be contributing to the drop in total bird population*, the newspaper says, *while a maturing landscape in inner-city has still allowed many individual species to grow in number*. Lifting the binoculars to my eyes. To the branches lifting sky. Wide and clear. Looking for. "The sky here is the same," says the woman who is here from the former Yugoslavia, she and her husband always say "former Yugoslavia," "the same as where I lived as a child in Africa. It's the same sky."

Surprised out onto the porch, snow falling, sparking. "Here," I say to the little girl from the former Yugoslavia, "let's feed your toy cat." Squatting on the edge of falling snow and she is 3 and asks her mother on the way to this party, "don't people speak here?" and I know she can't understand my English and I can't understand her Serbian, but we are squatting on the snow's edge, reaching our fingers, scooping snow, feeding it into the stuffed cat's pink mouth, laughing and laughing, until her mother sees her outside, doesn't see me, runs and carries her kicking and screaming inside, "She's not used to this cold, it's too cold for a child," and I remember her telling me about electricity shortages, food shortages, cold apartments in the former Yugoslavia, and I wonder about bombs exploding and running to make sure your children are alive and whole and your heart hammers and you refocus the binoculars for a close-up of a Downy Woodpecker exploring the grooves in the Cottonwood's bark, wishing you could discern the head of an owl barely moving, turning to look at you.

PLAIN AS THE EARTH shifting on its axis. The Winter Solstice, then one minute more sunlight each day. Wondering if our skin can tell, or the gland in our heads where light shines and tells our bodies to stop secreting the hormone that tells us to roll over in the morning and keep sleeping, keep sleeping. In and out of light, in and out of the trees. One more minute each day.

SURPRISED OUT OF SADNESS, out of watching my twin nieces Alex and Megan, almost two years old, pull off their own diapers, run and hurl themselves onto the floor, arms outstretched, rock naked on their tummies, laughing. Watch them dance and jump, fat baby legs, deep baby laughs. Their mother, my sister, in their muscles, in the shape of their fingers. Surprised into my sister and me at our Auntie's and Uncle's. My sister ("dister," my nieces say, "I love my dister") can't be more than two, hangs half-off the horse suspended on springs, one eyebrow cocked, me on the floor bucking, making her laugh and all the aunties and uncles have black hair. Into now, grey in our hair and the aunts and uncles shrinking, cousins growing fatter, and the lines in our faces I can hardly read moving in and out of all the cancers, deaths, births. In and out of trees.

PLAIN AS THE FOG LIFTING. A lake. Trees. Mountains. Hoar frost on the trees. Hoar frost sparkling in the sun. Alex and Megan laughing, running around the corner, "Boo," and my niece Mikaila already five and thin and our long talks on the phone. "It's so strange, Mik, seems like you were just a baby and I would hold you and wonder what you would be like when you were five, and before long you'll be ten, then fifteen."

"No, Berta, I don't want to be a teenager, ever." Yet someday I will be shrinking and she, they, will be walking down streets by themselves, opening car doors at night, kissing some man's or woman's ear, and "Be safe" is no longer enough, maybe never was, but oh this ache, this far-down deep ache for the safety of people I love eating oranges.

WANTING TO WRITE. Flush of crab-apples in autumn-light, outside my window. Deep red against green. The air sweet with apples apples apples. Rush of juice, bitter and sharp when I bite into one, up behind my jaw, simple as that. As taking another bite, each night the frost coming closer, the apples redder, the fuschia and lobelia and begonias dropping magenta & blue & ivory. The way the poplar leaves don't fall in the wind, but lift brilliant yellow into the sky, and even this yellow this sweetness this floating and flying and stroking and swallowing and holding weren't enough to stop the cancer from exploding in my friends' daughter's brain, yet I take another bite of crab-apple and hold four-year-old Alex's hand tight as we walk across the street to visit the tiny spruce tree she kneels in front of, wraps her arms around, kisses. "You can forgive a tree for pricking you," she says, her voice soft and her eyes half-closed, "if you love it enough." She picks up a yellow poplar leaf, wraps it around a branch of the spruce. "This is how you for-give a tree."

OR HER TWIN-SISTER, MEGAN. "I love animals, even dead ones." Her chubby four-year-old fingers slide a leaf under the piece of magpie we find by the park, lay another leaf over top. She scoops the bundle to her chest, pats the top leaf, "I'll just carry poor magpie for awhile, then I'll bury it and sing Jesus Loves Me." At home she slides the dead magpie or snake or sparrow or fish-head into a baggy, carries it around all day, talks to it, "Don't worry little snake, I love you." Holding a leaf, a hand, my friend holding her daughter. Alex holding stones, rubbing them over her cheeks, her eyes closed, "I love stones." My sister holding Alex and Megan when they were born and two pounds each and bright red and couldn't breathe without tubes and machines. Holding them now, plump and warm, before they get up and run, run among the trees.

Long After Fathers

I DREAM ABOUT YOU, DAD. NIGHT AFTER NIGHT after night.

I slip away from my bed, my body, into the black night. And there you are.

"I need to do this right," you tell me, pinching the aortas of your exposed heart. You ease the beating mass onto the table in front of you. "Everything has to be done just right."

"Yes," I say, my voice cool. "I'll help you." (Do I rest my hands on my hips or do I lounge against the table, watching you pinch, slice, snip?)

Your hands are small, transparent, white. We must talk, but I don't remember the words. I remember what's important. You operate on your own heart. I help.

"All done," you say at last, or I think you say. You pinch the aortas and raise the pulsing mass to the hole in your chest. Deftly you flick veins and arteries into place, smooth connections.

"You did it," I shout. "You did it."

Grinning, you step toward me. Or I step toward you. Grinning. The way we did when I came with you to your band rehearsals and you sang across the empty hall to me at the back, my eyes closed, concentrating on your voice floating out over the room, the meld of pitch and texture and emotion making my chest swell. "How was that?" you'd ask, and I would open my eyes to yours, serious on me, knowing that you would nod at my answer, sing the song again with my suggestions.

You raise a hand toward my shoulder. But stop suddenly. Your heart recoils into your ribs, shudders twice, then blows wide open.

I cradle your head in my arms as your voice fades. "What went wrong?" you cry. "What did I do wrong?"

THERE IS NO ALARM CLOCK. I cannot wake up from this dream.

A friend tells me what's revealing is the way I tell the story. I nod and say, "mmmh, yes I think you're right."

When I get home I tuck my head under the pillow in the spare bedroom. In my own bed I foetus-curl around my heart and rock back and forth.

"CANCER," Dr. Newton says, chewing his tongue. "Lymphoma. Stage four."

They pierce your hip with a thick long needle, ram the point into bone. No marrow, not even a congealed mass. So they bore out a piece of bone.

"Your body's destroying itself with its own immune system," Dr. Newton says, gently running his fingertips down your arm.

I'm fascinated by his hands – pillowed palms, fingers, brailing your arm for lumps. I know his daughter; she's my age. Brittle and coldly efficient. I can't put the two together, father and daughter.

"What a kind man," you say after he leaves. "Poor bugger having to tell me I have cancer." Your bottom lip trembles. Between us, empty bones splinter the air. I squeeze your wrist as if I can hold you together.

Put together, hold together, fathers, daughters. Blow the bloody mess to pieces and let me sift through the fragments.

This isn't a fiction. I have to bring you back so I can kill you peacefully. The way you wanted.

DON'T TELL DAD. Don't tell Dad. Don't tell Dad.

Rumbles in the belly of every family. Don't tell Dad. That Mom dyed her hair and it turned orange. When my brother woke up this morning his top sheet was all wet. My sister's growing bumps on her chest, nyah nyah nyah. My little brother, boy did he get drunk. The phone company called again – we're gonna cut off your phone if you don't pay your bill. But don't tell Dad.

Or worse – wait until I tell your father. Wait until your father gets home.

Oh God forgive us, we pray to him on the other side of the mountain, behind the bush. God made in the image of man, forever away at work. Forgive us forgive us we pray, pleading punishment. How lonely he must be when he comes home and faces his family's silent trembling.

Yet if he didn't shout so loud, I am your father, do as I say, we wouldn't be afraid would we? Would we?

The grade one teacher stops her class halfway through the Lord's Prayer. Gareth, you say it on your own, she says. Gareth bows his head, Our father who Art in heaven, Harold be thy name.

IN THE WRECK OF CHEMOTHERAPY, you lie on your back in Celeste's spare bedroom, chemicals leaching out your pores. You retch and sweat. I come and lie with you, lay my head on your chest. Your heart flutters and thuds against my cheek.

"Are you afraid of dying?" I ask.

"No," you say. "But I don't want to leave your mother. I've already broken her heart once, now I'm leaving her without a pot to piss in."

"She's forgiven you," I say. "We've all forgiven you. You need to forgive yourself."

"I can't," you say. "I can't. Your mother's a bigger person than I am."

Then you look at me, your eyes dazed with cancer and drugs. "She says she's quit smoking, but I know she's lying. I'm dying of cancer and she's going to kill herself smoking. Her mother died of asthma for Christ's sake, her father died of lung cancer. What the hell is she doing?"

I AM NINE.

You must be. Let me think. Nine plus nineteen equals...twenty-eight. Every morning you leave when it's still dark out.

In this house the floors are cold. "We need coal," you say. Lines squiggle across the linoleum like a million worms.

We catch grasshoppers in the field beside our house. Plop on the ground, our hands cupped together. Dddrrhh dddrrhh dddrrhh. The grasshoppers explode against our palms.

Mummy comes out with Captain Huff and Puff on her hip. "How many you got?" she asks. Celeste just shrieks and keeps chasing. She looks like a drunk troll. Alyd sneaks up real slow. His eyes are round. Plop. He carries the grasshopper close to his face. I have the jar because I'm the biggest. Mummy puts Captain Huff and Puff down. He giggles, then runs a few feet and flops on the ground. We all laugh because he doesn't know what he's doing. He laughs and snorts and does it again. We all laugh as long as we can.

I don't want to stop. I hate it here.

You are frowning when you get home so we don't tell you about Captain Huff and Puff and the grasshoppers. We don't tell you about Mummy singing I saw the li-i-ight into the light bulb either.

"Pratts are bringing down a tub tomorrow," Mummy tells you across the table.

"Yeah," you say, looking sideways at Celeste. "For Christ's sake," you say to her, "chew with your mouth shut."

Maybe you don't say that. Maybe you don't say anything. I don't remember what you say, just some of what you do. And what you don't say. ("Why do you remember the bad things?" Mom asks.)

You lead a black colt into our yard. He rears, lunges back. "Whoa, boy," you croon softly, "settle down boy, settle down boy."

His sides and your hair. Black in the sun. I can't take my eyes off him, you, as I move closer. You reach a hand to his sweat-matted neck. Your hand shakes. "He's yours," you say, without looking at me.

I'm fascinated by your hand, stroking, stroking, stroking.

"Where does he come from?" I ask.

You nod toward the mountain, miles across the valley. "Up the Adanac."

The colt snorts and jerks his head up.

"Up the Adanac." In the sun you and horse and mountain merge into one. I poke at a rock with the toe of my shoe. My heart stretches as big as Turtle Mountain, as big as the sun.

You leave on my sixteenth birthday. We sit around the long table waiting. "Gone to get his amps," Mom mutters. She bangs a cupboard door, stands with her back to us, her head down. "Shit." She stoops, yanks open the broiler door. "Goddamned steaks are goddamned burned." She slams the drawer shut.

"Maybe we should just eat without him." Agnes says, here with her daughter Tina.

"Yeah" Mom says, and bangs a dish of peas on the table. She rams her fork into the pieces of dark curled meat, slaps them on our plates. Alyd and Gareth stare at theirs but don't move to eat. Celeste looks out the window at the black hump of Turtle Mountain.

"Eat," Mom says. Her voice breaks.

Alyd and Gareth pick up their knives and forks. Celeste stares out the window. Her profile is sharp and pointy. I poke her thigh, but she ignores me. Mom waves her knife. "Goddammit Celeste, you eat or I'll break your bloody neck."

Celeste's face is iron.

"Do you hear me," Mom screams.

Celeste slides her eyes sideways. "I'm not eating this shit." She bites each word.

Mom lunges, right over Agnes and Tina. I can't see if she still has a knife. She grabs Celeste's shoulders, pushes.

Celeste's chair crashes backward, her head hits the floor.

Mom looks down at Celeste's face puckering, curls herself into a ball on the floor, a ripping sound comes out of her mouth.

"Stop," I scream. "Stop stop stop." I pull Mom's arm. The ripping sound grows louder and louder. Alyd and Gareth stare, their eyes wide. She starts to shake, her eyes flutter back. I slap her as hard as I can. Swing my arm and let her have it.

She looks as if she doesn't know who I am, then pulls me to her, her tears hot on my neck.

"Please leave him," we beg Mom when you come home months later.

You stop singing, sell the horses. "Jesus Christ woman," you snap whenever she tries to talk, "how can you be so bloody stupid?" In IDA Drugs in Blairmore, the woman who was your mistress brushes past. She clutches her hand to her chest like a broken claw. Spittle drools from the corner of her mouth. No one asks how you feel, and you don't tell.

THE SUMMER BEFORE I HIKE the West Coast Trail, I bring my friend Mary down to the Pass. "She's fifty-one," I tell you on the phone, "four years older than you."

"I learned to fly when I was sixteen," she tells you, and laughs. Then she tells you about the time her plane frosted up and she had to land in a farmer's field. "When I jumped out of my plane in a skirt, that farmer and his son started back as if they'd seen a ghost."

You laugh until your eyes run. Then you tell her about Lady Agnes MacDonald riding a cowcatcher through BC.

All night you trade stories. Most of them about the land, getting into the mountains. "I want to move up North," you tell her, "get away from all this." You point at the TV.

My knees shake as I climb the stairs to my old room. It was so much easier, Dad, when you were the villain. But I said I'd kill you peacefully, didn't I? I put it in writing.

ROSALIND, Dad tells you things. He confides in you. What did Dad say?

He wants to blow his brains out.

YOU, SICK WITH DREAD on the way to chemo, sitting for hours in the waiting room, swallowing, watching patients walk in with briefcases, pushed into the room in wheel-chairs, on hospital beds, hooked up to IV, people with hair, without hair, with skin yellow and thin and a haunted look in their eyes, chemicals so toxic the staff can't handle them with bare hands, drip into patients' veins, course through their bodies.

Into your veins, collapsing so the nurse has to poke and poke to find one that will take the needle, the burning chemicals. You sitting back in what looks like a dentist's chair, sweat beading your brow, trying to make conversation with the nurse and the doctor, trying to cheer them up, and the patients around you in their dentists' chairs, chemicals burning the insides of their veins, all of you wanting to see your children and grandchildren, friends and lovers a while longer.

You meeting the eye of the boy who comes in when you do, asking him how he is. "Leukemia," he tells you. "A musician," he tells you, and the two of you talk for hours about the sweetness of a Gibson guitar, a held note. On the drive home, already retching, you turn to me, your eyes red-rimmed, piercing. "It's not fair," you say, "he's just a boy, he should have a whole life ahead of him. At least I've experienced love and children. He's a kid, a child. If I could, I'd trade him places."

I FIND MYSELF PERCHED on the landing at the bottom of the stairs, two weeks before they carry you out for the last time, moaning, eyes running, wide-open, blind.

"Mom mom mom, please let me die." Your voice seeps out from under the bathroom door, dissolves into guttural sobs. The bathroom door clicks open. I press against the wall. You drag your bedroom-hidden carcass across the floor. Mom holds you under one arm and around your back. My chest begins to heave. I taste blood on my lip. Mom looks right at me. *Help me*, her eyes beg, *help me*. You turn your head to the wall. "Go to bed," you moan, "go to bed go to bed go to bed." Your voice dissolves. Your bedroom door clicks.

I press my forehead into the cool wall. The stench of blood and putrid flesh curls up my nostrils. Fragments past present and future swirl through the poison air. You in hospital, moaning and plucking at the green paper diaper they've wrapped you in. Your eyes stare in different directions. "Say hi to Roz," the nurse says, twisting your face toward me. You groan and wrench your head from her hands. Tears stream down your cheeks. You leaning against the wall in the polished corridor two days later. "What happened?" you ask, hardly able to keep your eyes open. "I have to know. I can't lose two days and not know." You tangled in your sheet at home, reaching for my hand, cancer exploding in your brain. "Get me out of here," you plead, "I'm going mad."

You you you. Around and around and around.

Stop. I thrust my arm into the swirling mass, drag out a picture of you with tubes stuck up your nose. I roll it between my fingers, worry it into a tiny hard pellet. One after another I pluck and worry. Hands full, I race upstairs. Flick on the lamp over your loading table. My husband sleeps in the dark across the room. Swiftly I roll the pellets into a cast-iron pot, plug in the hot plate. When the pellets begin to sizzle and melt, stinking of hot metal, I drop in a few more.

Past, present and future. You playing down by the Crowsnest River with your brothers. Your brother rests both hands on your bare shoulders. You squint sideways through dripping hair. You wrestling with Alyd on the lawn. You wear blue jeans and cowboy boots. Alyd wears swimming trunks. His face wears the same shy expression as yours. As mine. You sitting at table in a two-room shack in Bogusch's field, watching the sullen stranger who calls himself Da-back-from-war. He's wrapped in a grey blanket and he slurps his soup. Your mom glares at him from the counter. Suddenly she scrapes the cast-iron fry pan from the stove and bears down on the stranger, twisting the fry pan as if to show him inside and out. "You bastard," she roars, and smashes him over the side of the head.

You telling your boss to fuck off after he makes you union-exempt, then tries to bust the union so he can cut the pay of the women. You singing into a mike at the Hillcrest Miner's Club. Your Welsh voice fills every corner of the quiet hall. You curled on your side in hospital. Sometime between eight and eight-thirty a.m. you wheeze in the first half of a sigh. And hold and hold and hold.

Your grandchildren, born years after you die, their throats wide with laughter, wind in their limbs. One of them, ten years old, lifts the owl wings taped to her arms for the school opera, opens her mouth to sing. A woman in front of me turns to the woman next to her, tears in her eyes. "Oh," she says, "oh."

Another grandchild spreads her fingers over piano keys, another puts a saxophone to her lips, another lifts a bell to her shoulder, sends its bell voice out into the air, another dances his fingers over his guitar strings, the youngest at four walks up to an elderly stranger in a restaurant, "you have a beautiful face."

Past present and future. I melt them all together. Carefully I balance the casting ladle on the lip of the trembling iron pot. Then I blow dust out of the mould. Where do you keep the gas checks? In the right-hand drawer, in the right-hand drawer. Yes, I remember. I set the tiny brass cup to the right of the mould. Wipe my palm on my pant-leg. In one motion I grab, dip, pour. Fill completely on the first pour. Yes, I do I do. While the bullet cools in the mould, I fiddle with the press. Crank the handle. Forward – closed. Backward – open. Dump the bullet shining silver onto a piece of flannelette. Press gas check onto bottom of bullet. Hold between the open jaws of the press. Crank – forward forward forward. Beautiful. Lube lube. I squeeze a black grease-stick into a fine groove running the circumference of the bullet. Crank – backward backward backward. The bullet thuds onto the flannelette, sharp and clean. Now prime the brass. Where…? Yes, left-hand drawer. I slide the drawer out smoothly. Twelve empty cylinders stare up at me. I fit a cool brass cylinder onto the primer cup. Squeeze together in the press. Now charge the brass. What…? How…? Which rifle will you use? Yes, the .30-06 Gareth made you out of bird's-eye maple. I reach for a tin that reads Smokeless Powder 4831. Pop the lid off. The can sends up a fine sweet dust like human ash. I measure out 56 grains on a miniature balance scale. Shake them into the brass. Nearly full – a fast burn. At last I pick up the bullet. It is hot against my palm. I slide it slowly into the mouth of the brass. Bullet and brass – a complete shell. With a sharp pin I carve into the bullet a horse, a mountain, the sun, and your name.

You walk out to the truck on your own. "God the air smells sweet," you say as we climb the old hoist road. You breathe slowly, deeply. The tip of Turtle turns red in the rising sun. Past the old mine works.

"I remember the miners' lamps bobbing up here in the morning," you say, "bobbing down at night." You chuckle.

"Remember the time we rode up here on Easter and Chief, and saw those two bears sun-tanning?" I ask.

"Yeah." You shake your head. "And coming down you somersaulted backward off Chief. I thought you'd broke your neck."

"I remember," I say, "you made me lie still while you felt every bone in my body."

The red flush slips down over the brow of Turtle. The valley opens out on our left. You nod across the valley toward the Adanac. "I remember walking miles with that wild bugger Tar Baby shying and rearing. The only thing I could think was, God, make her love this horse."

"I did," I say, and we laugh.

I stop the truck before we get to Grassy Clearing. We get out together; you carry the gun. "Do you want me to walk you to Grassy?" I ask, rolling a rock with the toe of my shoe.

You don't answer for a long time. "No," you say at last, your voice low. Then you hug me and pat my back. "I love you," you say, then turn and walk away.

I sit in a clump of sweet grass long after the shot echoes through the valley. Long after the sun descends over the humped back of Turtle Mountain.

SOLANGE

Fly Away Home

Lady bug lady bug
Fly away home
Your mother is drunk
Her kids are alone

– Where are you going?
– None of your business.
The ladybug scratches the back of my hand. She is red, redder than me, redder than my redhead mother running lipstick over her mouth.
– I'm not making dinner again. Marla can do it.
– Do as you please.
The ladybug lifts her wings, walks toward my thumb, trailing two transparent black tails. I blow on her, softly. She stops, pulls her wings together. One crisp husk over her back.
– I'm glad you're never home.

I concentrate on my ladybug. Pick her up gently, her body brittle against my thumb and finger. There, I set her on the windowsill in the corner where I find all the others in a pile. Dead husks bright red.

The kitchen door bangs. Outside, my mother's red head crosses under the window. Her curls jerk and she walks carefully carefully down the hill, down the straight grey line to the Bellevue Legion, grey in the sun where she will drown the voices in her head telling her to kill us.

— Where are you going?

— None of your business.

Marla stands behind me in the kitchen. I lean over the mirror, draw a blue line around my right eye.

— Can I come?

— Nope. You have to make supper for Brad and Lyla.

I reach across to my left eye. Without blinking I can see Marla's wide-open brown eyes, my hand tracing my eye in the mirror.

— I don't know where they are.

— They'll come when they're hungry.

THE DAIRY ROAD runs straight down the hill, all the way downtown. I walk slowly, scuff my shoes over our new sidewalks. I pass Cates's grey house, two half-tons in the driveway, Ron and his dad home in the same house, same day, eyes and nails rimmed with coal.

Over white arborite in a white kitchen, too much light, they blink at each other.

My older brother Martin has silver-sage eyes.

Past old Stezics' house, pink and green against the cliff. Through the whole war, he said, my wife and I and the boy, we make it safe through the whole war, and we come here and what happens, we go icefishing, I turn my back, and the boy disappears through the ice. What kind of God lets that happen?

Martin's father has brown eyes.

Past Todesco's house, white and brown, sideways in their yard inside their caragana hedge. Two daughters, only Sappho has her mother's big breasts. The boys lounging outside the café stare at them, all the way down Main Street. Sappho's head high, her eyes glassy. Someday, she says, I'll teach my breasts ventriloquism. Yellow caragana flowers will soon tighten into pods, burst their seeds.

Over our table my eyes watch Martin's eyes not watching our father who does not live here anymore. Mine are silver-sage, like Martin's. Like our mother's. Martin and I and Marla and Brad and Lyla. We used to share the same father.

Chin up, I try to see in the windows of the Kosa's house, dark and sleepy under a giant spruce. She has black hair to her waist. He rides broncs. They have been married one week and their dog has cancer, a lump under one teat, square and stupid under my square, stupid fingers. No light, no movement.

I walk slow, but I'm not slow like they say, not like Brad.

Down Dairy Road people turn into the ball park, cushions under their arms. I knock on Corine's door across from the park. Corine whispers as we cross the street.

– Roland's playing today. I asked Tony.

– So?

I follow her out of the sun into the new brown stand, almost full on Saturday afternoon. The people in the stands smile at Corine, Mrs. Todesco with her big teeth, Mrs. Smelyk, old Mrs. Dobrin, Mr. Beard, Cy Ramsay, smile and smile and smile. At Corine.

– You missed one of ours, girls. Pop fly. John Palka.

They look through me, too pale, too thin, moves slow. We sit in the middle of the stands, my thigh next to old Mrs. Dobrin's, her dress flowered orange and black. Smells like moth balls. Chin up I search through the screen for Roland behind home dugout.

He picks up two bats, swings them forward, around, back. Forward, around, back. Bellevue's second batter stands, legs apart, tense at the plate, but I watch Roland swing in front of the rocks rising up the hill behind the dugouts. Forward, around, back. Below his cap his hair lifts, brushes his neck, lifts. My hands curl palm-up on my thighs.

The ball arches over left field, eclipses the sun, floats floats, down into a waiting glove.

– C'mon guys, two down, only two down.

– Atta boy, Rollie, show these clowns what we can do, Rollie.

– Make it a big one, Rollie, big guy. Show your stuff, big guy.

Roland throws one bat into the tall grass behind the dugout, strolls to home plate, spreads his legs. He bats left. I watch his back, his buttocks tense under his uniform. I watch his eye, blue and white, from the side. I am invisible behind the screen, invisible under the sky. He stares at the pitcher, at the sun, at the black shape moving up Dairy Road.

– Put 'er here big buddyyy. Put 'er here big buddyyy. Easy batter big buddyyy, easy batter.

The back-catcher bounces in his squat, ignores the black Mercury rolling by the park beyond centre field. My fingers clench, square and stupid, nails curled up instead of down. *Go away.*

The pitcher breathes on the ball, leans back in slow motion, leg up, arm back. I blink at Roland, a black spot rolling into my eye. *Go away.* The pitcher lunges forward.

The ball arcs over second, ricochets off the front fender of the black Mercury crashing through the wood and mesh fence, rolling into centre field. Long and black, two fins terrible behind.

– What the?

– Who's the crazy asshole?

– Get the hell outta there buddy.

I blink but the car rolls over second, past players, legs spread, gloves hanging against their thighs.

– What the?

The Blairmore pitcher moves slow motion off the mound toward first base.

The black car rolls over the infield, onto the pitcher's mound, and stops.

Corine looks at me, but I keep my head straight, stare at the black fins. Beside me Mrs. Todesco's breath sucks in, blows out. All around me noisy breathing. From the field, silence. My nails dig into my palms.

The driver's door flings open, a black figure springs out, lands feet apart. Black leotards, black undershirt, black cape, black mask. A bulge in the leotards.

Fly away
Fly away
Fly away home
Your wife is pissed
Your kids are alone

He jumps toward the stands, lifts his cape.

– Holy baseball Robin. We've found them.

Around me, silence. I swallow my father's voice.

– Now what Robin? What do we do with them?

He crouches, spins, leaps toward first base, his cape fluttering, voice shouting.

– You think you fooled me, villains, but I was watching, I was watching. Batman sees all.

Around first, onto second, his skinny legs churning.

– Right under my nose, right under my nose. Thought I wouldn't see. But haha, Batman sees everything.

Around second, running for third, arms flung back, shouting, his voice echoing off the limestone boulders behind the dugouts.

– Holy villains, slime-pickers, piss-drinkers. Thought you could hide them, didn't you, didn't you?

Faster, around third, flying for home plate, shouting.

– But never never never. I'm Batman. Batman comes in the night. I'm Batman. Batman.

He crosses home plate. Around me, laughing, clapping, chattering.

– He's drunk, the stupid bastard's drunk.

He raises his fists.

– I will save this holy shit world, for you. I AM BAT MAN.

MY FEET KNOW THESE ROCKS, my toes curl around bumps, sharp points. From behind and below, voices rise up out of the park.

– Pitch 'im out big Rollie, pitch 'im out big buddyyy.

– Easy batter, Rollie, chicken-shit batter big guy.

– Put 'er here big buddyyy. Put 'er here big buddyyyy.

After the rocks, a meadow of long yellow grass and thistle. I step into the grass and the voices drop into a murmur. My shins know this grass, quick slices at my skin. I walk to the middle of the meadow, where the sink-hole grows grass short and green. From here, on my side, I look up the last ridge between Bellevue and the world. Rocks and trees and cliffs and a black gash of coal.

In the same house, in their white kitchen, Ron and his father black around the eyes, blink at each other.

And at the bottom of the hill – the old hoist house, oily wheels and cables. A man hanged himself there, years ago. His son came looking for him in his truck. He hanged himself, too, years later after he was married and had kids.

Then there's Larry's dad. Put a shotgun in his mouth and pulled the trigger. Blew off his bottom jaw. I saw him at a wedding dance in the Catholic Hall, his mouth always open. Larry doesn't talk about him.

Muffled cheers rise over the rocks into my meadow. His legs in leotards, his bulge that has something to do with what I am, with Brad and Lyla and Marla and Martin. Martin goes crazy when he drinks, drives through Frank Slide playing chicken, can't stop grinning.

But leotards, and a cape, and a party mask. I am Batman.

I am.

I laugh until my side hurts and Hoist Hill swims against the sky.

Solange

SOLANGE, NOT HER REAL NAME, NO FRENCH IN her, not one drop. Red-head drinking mother, red-head drinking father. In her pulsing carotid, thick burgundy blood whooshes washes every second through her soft tissue.

Keeps this name, Solange, "So" a hint a sigh a beginning, "Lange" barely a touch, a whisper of silk, of satin, of soft cotton on her soft her private. Keeps this name sewn just so, Solange, on a wisp of white silk in her back pocket.

Steers with one hand, Solange, so much like "So long, it's been good to know ya" or in French "Sol Ange," earth angel. In her rusted Rambler, she drives through the dark, away from Bellevue in the mountains, away from her red-head mother, her sisters, her brothers. Solange, warm and safe and breathing inside her car, inside the dark, on a road sinewing through the foothills, dark mounds and dark curves. Away.

Safe, you are safe Solange, slide your free hand into your back pocket, cup the soft silk against your round, your mound, your curve. Take deep breaths, Solange, your mouth open, deep into your lungs.

Own the dark, Solange. Your legs against the seat, your hand on the wheel, your foot on the pedal, your fingers loving your silk.

Trees, Solange, those naked white limbs out of the dark in your headlights. Aspens. Lodgepole Pines. Tree knots black and woody. Branches, those are branches, not arms waving at you to stop, stop Solange, stop. Branches, Solange, branches. Wood. And rocks under the tires, they are rocks, just rocks, glacial till scraped and rolled and scraped. Not heads, Solange, or finger bones or knee caps.

Yet. What if? What if your mother, walking jerky in the dark, singing, "You take the high road and I'll take the low," her silver-sage eyes blinking and confused?

What if your father, his brown eyes when he lived with your mother and sisters and brothers and you, before you went away, in the house on the hill. His eyes when he drove his black Mercury onto the ball park in Bellevue, jumped out dressed in black leotards and a cape and flew around the bases shouting, "I am Batman, Batman."

What if your brother Martin, eyes silvery-sage, half-closed, always smiling when he's drunk?

What if, Solange, what if Brad or Lyla, so thin so scruffy and their eyes so lost?

What if any one of them under your tires, the crunch of their bones?

Oh Solange, walks the ditches, the wind whips her hair, snatches vowels from her mouth. Swings her foot ahead of her in the dark, dreads the soft thud of her boot on flesh. Fingers the soft silk in her pocket, her heart pounding.

Headlights slice the dark, light up aspens, pine, grass, rocks. Solange falls face-down in the ditch. "Don't stop, please don't stop." She clutches grass and dirt and rocks. A half-ton whizzes by. Solange gets up in the dark, brushes off her legs, kicks along the ditch.

Rocks, Solange, those are rocks under your tires. Don't think about Marla, her soft brown eyes. Don't think your mother, her face like yours. Don't think their eyes, their bones, under your tires.

Think, rock, Solange, limestone, glacial till. Stop doing this, Solange, stop and go back to your car, drive into Calgary, enter your apartment in the dark, Corine and Janice asleep in their bedrooms, undress in the living room by the streetlight, slide between your sheets on the couch, and sleep.

Solange.

Oh Solange.

Shivers all night along the ditches, one side then the other, into the trees. Who knows how far a body. All night, her knees tremble, her breath shallow in the wind, uphill, down, kicking, probing, until lemon on the horizon, new light through the trees. Aspen and pine. Rocks on the road, rocks and twigs and grass in the ditches.

Staggers back to her rusted Rambler, cold in her skin, her bones, down her long legs and arms. Drives into Calgary, shivering, both hands on the wheel.

Sinews her body, teeth chattering, between her sheets.

IN THE TINY KITCHEN of her apartment, sun drifting in the window, drifting on her bare arms, Solange stretches her arms over her head, arches her back. Yawns, sun on her face, through her peach nightie.

Solange, her fingernails square and flat, but her fingers long and peach, slides four slices of bacon from the plastic wrapper, lays them side-by-side in the hot pan, licks her fingertips. While the bacon pops and sizzles, she stretches between the fridge and toaster. Her nightie flutters against her nipples, her stomach, her thighs.

While the bacon pops and sizzles, the toast lies in the sun on the counter, four bright red tomato slices, Solange stands in the bathroom in front of the mirror, head slightly back, red hair caressing her long peach neck, smiles, so-so Solange, eyes half-closed. In four hours Corine and Janice, also from Bellevue, will come home to this shared Calgary apartment, but right now she is alone, with the smell of bacon and her nightie fluttering and her silver-sage half-closed eyes. She licks the tip of each finger, watches the tip of each finger run by her small peach lips, over the tip of her tongue. Inhales deeply the scent of bacon, toast, ripe tomato, Corine's perfume, Secret underarm deodorant, Avocado bath oil, lifts her arms, slides the neck of her nightie up over her face, inhales her own sweet dark must, slides the nightie up her long thighs, her waist, her breasts. Smiles at herself.

Oh Solange, Solange, you are transforming, flowering, a touch a sigh a beginning.

Slides into the tub, slides down into warm Avocado over her legs, soft red thatch, round mound, peach nipples, sighs, eyes closed, nibbles the hot bacon plump tomato buttery toast.

Oh Solange, mmmmmmmmmm Solange, as if, as if slow fluttering from a chrysalis.

"Two ADULTS."

"Two adults, two children."

"One student."

"One senior."

They slide their money into the cool tin dip under the glass. Solange's peach fingers settle on bills, coins, slide them smooth over the counter into the till, slide the tickets across and into the cool tin dip. Head tilted back, red hair shining under the light, keeps her eyes partly closed, slow half-smile for each woman, each man, each child, slow smile for her own reflection inside the glass.

Slow half-smile for the looks in their eyes when they see her there, notice her, red and peach and silvery shining. Notice her and blush or lean toward the glass or look away, look back as they walk away. Notice her, all of them, how could they not? Willowy, sinewy Solange. And sometimes a man who came on his own or with friends or with a woman, waits until the line-up has gone, leans close to the slits in the glass made so she can hear their voices, looks earnestly into her eyes, "Can we meet?" "Can I take you out after?" "I need to find out who you are." "This might sound like a line, but you're the most beautiful woman I've ever met." And Solange, oh Solange, lays her head farther back, smooth and slow, stretches her long neck, reaches into her back pocket, runs her soft white silk through her fingers, mouths "Midnight."

After the movie starts, she stands, stretches, flicks her fine red hair off her collar, climbs the stairs to the foyer, drifts into the aroma of popcorn, hot butter. The others watch her, tall and sinewy, cross the floor, lights in her red hair.

Oh Solange, drift behind the counter, fill the popcorn maker, pour oil into the hanging pot. Reach into your back pocket, run your name, So Lange, smooth and silky through your fingers. Head slightly back, smile a gracious smile at the women and the men filling the plastic slots with licorice, Smarties, chocolate bars, smile at them watching you, wanting you.

Oh a touch a sigh a beginning.

Or, so long, good-bye, see you, au revoir.

Au revoir Bellevue, small town in the mountains. Au revoir mountains and limestone boulders beside the highway and Mother, Father, Martin, Lyla, Brad.

Au revoir, two years in the Bellevue Theatre, Friday and Saturday evenings. *She, what's her name, what's her name again? That girl, that skinny red-head in the lobby, you know the one, stringy red hair, hands and feet like a big puppy. You have to feel sorry for her, chumming around with Corine Patinek, Corine so blonde and curvy.*

Jesus, that skinny one, what the hell's her name, I can see her plain as day behind the counter there in the Bellevue Theatre, hell she spills at least one pop a night, usually on her own blouse or shoe. Never looks you in the eye, either, ducks her head forward or lays it back and closes her eyes. Bit slow I think, if you know what I mean. No damn wonder, with those two for parents. Took off to Calgary, I hear, working at a show-hall there.

Here in the city Solange smells the popcorn, heat of the popper in her cheeks, rubs her soft silk name. Slow smiling drifts between the popper and candy counter, slide boxes and bags into their slots. Drifts down the front steps to her glass booth for the second show.

Drifts down the back stairs at 11:30, into the alley. Slides into her rusted Rambler. One hand on the wheel, the other cupped in her back pocket, she steers through the downtown streets, under street-lights and office lights. You are Solange now, in the city now. Hum a song Solange, hum a city song.

Oh Solange, the beauty of it, shimmer of lights at night, strangers on the street, a silk soft name and you, emerging, shimmering. C'est belle, Solange, très très belle, mon amour.

The man who has sat through two movies or gone out for coffee for three hours alone or taken his girl-friend home then driven back downtown, waits for you outside the empty theatre, checks his watch, crushes a cigarette with his toe, turns up his collar, peers through the glass door across the vestibule into your empty booth, rattles the door, kicks a parking metre.

He is waiting for you, Solange, has been waiting for you forever. This moment, his whole existence, focused on you. He will come back and you will give him the same slow smile you give every man, woman, child and he will ache, you will see in his eyes, or he will curse you, every rage he's ever felt aimed at you, Solange, and you will see that too in his eyes, and you will smile, so-so Solange, so smooth.

Listen to the rattle of your engine, Solange, you are almost home in this city. Silk in your pocket, name curving your cheek. See the Louise Bridge ahead of you, Solange, one smooth arching bridge over the Bow River, the river an opaque sinew so dark and smooth you could walk on it. Listen to the rattle of your engine, hum through your thighs.

Forget rocks under your tires, Solange, forget their bony crunch. Rocks. Look at the river down there, smooth and black and lights shimmering, red green orange white.

Rocks, Solange, city stones, city pebbles, city gravel. Don't think of limestone boulders, Solange, ninety million tons on both sides of the highway through the Frank Slide in the mountains. Don't think of your red-head mother in the dark wandering drunk on the edge of the highway. Her head jerks with each step. Where, where did it go, her face? Her own face, she had a face she used to recognize in the dark, if she could find where it went. Where she went, looking for herself in the dark. Her head jerks, teeth rattle. "Could you help," she shouts at the boulders black and solid along the highway, "could you help me, I seem to have lost something?"

Solange, oh Solange, don't think of your red-head mother alone in the dark, don't see her stagger, trip, reach out for a boulder in the dark, "help me, can you help me." Don't think of how hard a rock, how hard the fender of a car, how brittle your mother's bones.

Drive, Solange. Cross this bridge, Solange, almost home in this city. Tiny rocks. Pebbles. Don't think of her forehead against cold limestone, her skinned knuckles in her mouth, "help me, I'm lost, oh I'm lost." Don't listen for the catch in her throat, her moan, "help me, Solange. You look the way I used to, Solange, can you help me find who I was."

Keep going, Solange, don't stop.

Every pebble makes a crunch, you can't stop in the middle of a bridge in the middle of a city.

So many rocks beside the river in the dark. So many rocks worn smooth. So many rocks under your shoes, smooth and cold and wet under your fingers as you squat, feel for the eye sockets, the unhinged bottom jaw.

THEY WAIT FOR MARTIN in his green half-ton to come get them for the party. A Crowsnest party here in Calgary. Corine and Janice and Rosalind, who lives in an apartment across the street, and Solange, green eye-shadow, shiny peach lips, red hair curled under, green mohair sweater.

They wait for him, lights out, in the tiny living room, Janice and Corine on the couch, Solange's sheets heaped on the arm, Rosalind cross-legged on the floor, streetlamp light on her small face, shadows in her eyes. And Solange, Solange, lounges on a chair beside the sliding-glass doors, cool on her cheeks, away from the smell of Bellevue in Corine's hair, on Janice's skin, grief over Bellevue in Rosalind's voice.

"When are you going back?"

"When he decides." Corine, so blonde in Bellevue, laughing, head back, in Bellevue, walking up the middle of the Dairy Road, head high, sighs here in Calgary, runs a shaking hand through her hair, avoids Rosalind's eyes.

"You mean there's a chance he might say no?" Rosalind's voice low in the dark, Bellevue in her voice. Oh Solange, watch and listen, but don't get drawn in. Corine will go back, Janice will go back, you can smell it on them, but Rosalind you don't know, she could still drop out, the only one at university, only two months into her first year, she could still sell her books, hitch a ride back to Bellevue. Watch her, watch Rosalind, the only one who calls you by your old name, the name you left in the house on the hill, with your mother and sisters and brothers. Watch she doesn't trap you in one of the stories she has begun writing about Bellevue.

Stretch on your chair, Solange, stretch your arms over your head, bury your nose in your mohair, breathe in musk-oil, think about the party, think about their eyes, all the guys from high school who didn't see you just last year, looked right through you in the hall at school, at parties up the bush behind town, watching you here in Calgary. Tonight at the party, they will want you. Stretch, feel the warm current in your groin.

"No bloody way, not after my father talks with him." Corine laughs, avoids the shadows in Rosalind's eyes, picks at a nub on her sweater. "It's not that he doesn't want to marry me, he has to get used to the idea. He wants kids, he just needs time for it to sink in." She tosses her head, street-lamp light in her blond hair. "Right, Solange? You hung around with us. You know he's not like other guys."

Corine's bright eyes in the street-lamp light, bright and sparking in the Bellevue Theatre when the guys from Coleman drive to Bellevue to watch a show, flirt with Corine over the counter. "What, Blondie, I drive all the way from Coleman and you give me popcorn? Me and a bunch of guys are having a party later, the old man's away, you wanna come? I'll give you a ride." Their eyes watching Corine, watching her laugh, toss her head, her blond hair sparking under the bright light. Watch her creamy hands, her breasts under her white blouse, high and round. Watch her red lips, "Sorry Sweetheart, I already got a ride home." Their eyes never leaving Corine, not once flickering to her standing right next to Corine, so close she can smell Corine's herbal shampoo, even when they say, flicking their heads but not their eyes, "Aw come on, Corine, bring your friend along." And Corine tosses her head, looks sideways at her, "Sorry, my friend and me have other plans." Corine laughs, mutters under her breath, "Help me get rid of him,

Lorne'll kill me." Laughs when Lorne picks them up in his black half-ton in front of the show-hall. Sits in the middle, one thigh touching Lorne's, the other touching hers, whispers, "We'll drive you home, but if my dad asks, you spent the whole night with us." Around the block, up the Dairy Road, Corine's perfume, Lorne's hockey sweat.

Corine turns the radio up, closes her eyes, hums to the music. Lorne drives, eyes straight ahead. Past the ball park, past Corine's house, until they are climbing the steep hill to Solange's house, her house and her red-head mother's, her sisters' and brothers'. At the bottom of the hill Corine snuggles up to Lorne, puts her lips on his neck, whispers "How are ya?" Presses against his side, waves at her sliding out of the truck, "See you tomorrow. Be at my house by 10:30, I have something to tell you."

Oh Solange, forget stepping over the dog, pushing open the door, the numbness in your hands. Forget Marla's breathless voice in the kitchen, dirty dishes on the counter, the table, fridge, floor, stench of mold, old meat. "He's doing it again, Martin's playing chicken again in the Slide. He was drunk so I went with him, we almost hit three cars head-on, I couldn't stop him, he grins and grins, says he's going out again, you have to go get her out of the Legion, tell her to come home."

Solange, Solange, forget Brad and Lyla, always skinny and scruffy and no expression on their faces, in their voices, out playing who knows where 11 o'clock at night.

Reach into your back pocket, run your silk-white name through your peach fingers. So Lange, hint sigh beginning, a chrysalis. Sigh, yes sigh, Solange, stretch, your red hair gleaming in the light, stretch, roll your shoulders, smile, oh your peach lips your sleepy silver-sage eyes, smile at Rosalind so serious on the floor, Corine on the couch, her eyes bright, Janice beside her, plump and silent.

Who stands up, "Jesus Christ, this isn't a funeral. I'm going to make some coffee. Anyone want coffee?"

Oh Solange, this moment, this unfurling, this hanging bright and shimmering in the air. Hang on, Solange, hang on.

MARTIN PARKS FACING THE WRONG WAY, so they go round to the street to get in. Corine slides in first, then Janice. Rosalind perches on Janice's knee. At last Solange slides in and pulls the door closed.

Over top Corine's and Janice's and Rosalind's heads, Martin grins at her, slow sleepy grin, "Ready?" The smell of rye, musk, rose. Martin's eyes like hers, mouth like hers. Solange lays her head back slowly, grins slowly, "Ready."

The truck growls, jumps forward. Rosalind grabs for the dash, jerks back against Janice. Janice turns her face toward Solange, "Jesus Christ." And Martin, red hair peach skin half-closed silver-sage eyes, grins and grins. Grins at the headlights shooting for them, careening, whizzing past. Grins at the horns blaring at them, the fingers and fists raised at him.

Solange, half-close your eyes, grin at the lights flying by, smile at Martin's grinning profile. Oh Martin.
Martin Martin. Looks just like your mother when he
gets drunk, so you don't have to.

SOLANGE ON THE BIG ARM-CHAIR sips her tall rye
and Pepsi. Dips her head forward, a small smile, lays
her head back, eyes closed. Janis Joplin's gravely voice
throbs out the stereo speakers on either side of the
room.

She opens her eyes, smiles at the room swimming
in blue light, swimming in a haze of grass and booze.
Smiles at two guys and two girls, long straight hair
parted in the middle, passing around a joint. The girl
with the joint, brown shiny hair, black eyeliner, what's
her name, she was a cheerleader, father owns the
hardware in Blairmore, money and piano lessons and
skating lessons. Takes a toke, sighs, smiles at her,
Solange, red and peach and green and shimmering.

And the guys, Solange, look how they watch you,
look how the ones who never saw you before, looked
right through you on the streets of Coleman,
Blairmore, Bellevue, looked through you at parties, in
the hallways, basketball games, show-halls, looked
right through you. Watch their eyes find you here in
the corner of the room, find your deep red hair, your
sleepy silver-sage eyes, your slow smile. Watch their
eyes keep finding you, all night, coming back to you,
you Solange, as they pour drinks, flirt with the pop-
ular girls, toke, banter with the other guys. Watch.

Solange takes another sip, runs her tongue over her lips. Soon they will come to her, sit in a circle around her, all the guys and the girls, will move close to her. Time, it's a matter of time.

For now she watches the long hair and jeans and pale faces in the blue light. Corine and Janice stand by the table with the booze. Corine looks into her glass, her white hair falls forward, curtains her face. Her hand so creamy around the plastic glass, her nails red. She takes a quick sip. Gin, Solange, Corine here in Calgary drinking gin, taking quick sips. Corine pushes her hair back from her face, her eyes shift around the room. One of the Coleman guys raises his eyebrows, walks toward her. She drops her head forward, a quick sip.

Oh, Solange, look how Corine shifts her weight side-to-side, runs her fingers through her hair, sips, and looks around to see where you are. Look how she moves closer to Janice, sips, looks for you.

Oh Solange, remember Corine this summer, down by the river in Bellevue. Eight of you down by the river, sitting on logs around a fire, the others necking. And you sitting legs stretched out beside Roland. All the guys older, all the guys from Bellevue, they all play hockey and baseball. All the girls know how to banter, when to laugh, except you.

Orange from the fire in her hair, in her eyes, Corine drinks slow from a bottle of lemon gin. Her left hand slides up Lorne's thigh. Shadows flicker under her chin, her nose, her eyes. She stands, "I need to find a tree. Come with me, Solange." For the first time, calls you Solange. Walks away from the fire into the dark, knows you will follow. Cool river-damp embraces you as you follow her crashing through the aspens, "Oh God, I can hardly hold it. Hurry, Solange, I want to get back to the fire, and my sweetie." You shiver, loud laughter behind you. A rustle of clothing and Corine's dark shape squats. "Do the same," she says, "I wanna talk to you." You drop your jeans, squat, cool damp on your buttocks. "Listen, Solange," Corine whispers, fierce and fast, "at least Roland came out with you tonight, you've been in love with the guy for years, the least you could do is smile. It doesn't matter that you're going away for awhile, hell I'm going for as long as it takes me to do my Nursing Aid, but at least I got something to come home to. You gotta lighten up, laugh at Roland's jokes a bit, move closer to him. Don't just sit and stare in the goddamn fire. Don't be too easy, but at least make him think you might like it."

Back beside the fire, heat of the fire in their faces, Corine whispers in Lorne's ear, her cheeks flushed. One of the guys get up, grabs a girl's hand. They get into a truck, drive just out of the fire's light, stop. Solange watches from the corner of her eye. The brake light pulses red, black, the truck engine stops. She bends forward, picks up a piece of bark, throws it on the fire. Sparks crackle up into the night. On the other side of the fire a couple slide onto the ground, press together. Corine laughs softly. Rustle of clothing, deep wet of river, a sigh, skin, heat from the fire, a male voice moans. Heat from the fire up her shins, her thighs. Solange looks at Roland's flushed cheeks, blue eyes staring at the fire, leans toward his ear, "Want to go for a walk?" Scent of Irish Spring soap, his skin, warm and flushed, so close she can almost taste it. "Yeah." He stands.

Beside the river Roland bends, heaves a rock high into the air. Solange tries to see it against the black sky, waits for the deep phloop. He bends and hurls, bends and hurls. She shivers, curls her flat stupid fingers into her pockets, watches his black shape bend and throw. She takes a deep breath, "Why do you hang around with them then?"

"To show her I don't give a goddamn." His shoes scrape against rocks, his arm she can't see whizzes through the air.

The cold, the river, her shoulders shake. Used to this, she is used to this. Knows what happens next. He moans, turns in the dark, presses her back against a tree, presses his body hot and shaking against her. His lips, his breath. His tongue between her lips, "I don't want to hurt you." Presses his groin into hers. "I can't help it, I love her, I love her." Presses. Pushes. His lips in the dark hot on her throat, his hands up under her bra, his fingers on her nipples. "Go away," he whispers, hot breath on her face, "go away and do your journalism. You deserve better than this." He rubs his groin against hers, up and down. She wraps one leg around him, pulls him tighter. His hard groin through her pants. Rubbing, pushing. She opens her legs wide. "You. Deserve. Better." He shudders, kisses her eyelids in the dark. Her heart pounds, her groin aches.

But that was before, Solange, before you, Solange, before you drove away from your red-head drinking mother, your sisters and brothers stuck in Bellevue, your father already long gone. Before you, your white silk name, your chrysalis, your red peach silvery shimmering. Shimmering. Stretch, Solange, smile so so slow, a slow sip. Your throat long and cool. Look at Rosalind, so small, so smart, leaning against the wall, Malcolm who goes to university leaning over her, his face so sincere. And you know what he says. "I like you, Rosalind, I really do. I can talk to you. You seem to understand. But I still love Sharon, I can't help it. She had to go to university in another city, she has to see other guys. I understand. I can wait." You know they will disappear to his apartment, lie on the living room carpet in the dark, his breath sweet on her face all night, "I like you, Rosalind. You're sweet, you're smart. But I just can't get her out of my system, I can't let go. I think about her all the time."

You know, because tomorrow Rosalind will sit shivering and hungry on your closed toilet while you lounge in your hot Avocado bath nibbling your hot bacon and tomato. You will offer her a bite, a whole sandwich, a piece of meat-loaf from the fridge, a slice of tomato, anything. She will shake her head, "Can't, I ate too much yesterday," and stare as you sink your teeth into the bacon and your mouth fills with warm salt and butter. Stare as you nibble, chew with your head back against the tub, and tell you how Malcolm recited poetry in the dark, how her mother and father are back together but her father won't talk to her on the phone even when she begs her mother to put him on, how Malcolm's studying geology but he recited a poem about fish, flesh, and fowl, and the young in one another's arms, and an old man who sails away from all this to a holy city where he becomes a golden bird. And you will look into her deep blue eyes with the black circles around her irises, dark shadows underneath, you will look in her eyes, smell the cold black seeping out of the mine in the coulee below her house in Bellevue, and your shoulders will shiver, you will sink lower into the tub, sink deeper into warm Avocado. You will close your eyes, take a deep deep breath, sigh, take a slow bite.

Oh, take a slow sip, Solange, half-close your silver-sage eyes, look and don't look at Luigi on the other side of the room, Luigi sitting cross-legged under a blue fish-net draped from the corner to a light near the middle. Look how he talks to that girl with her long black hair, high-waisted checkered pants, black blouse open at the neck. Luigi is talking with her, but he watches you, Solange, talks with his hands, lays his head back, laughs, leans toward her, his round brown eyes so serious on you, Solange, looking over her left shoulder. Watch how she shakes her head, her long black hair swings back and forth over her white throat. His eyes on you, Solange, see how Luigi nods his head toward the ceiling. Solange, shake your head, just a tiny move-ment, your shimmering red hair brushes your neck, give him a slow sleepy smile over the rim of your glass.

Lay your head back, eyes smooth and slow, so Solange, as Luigi and the girl get up off the floor, weave between people drinking, toking, laughing, weave toward you, here on this couch in this blue air. Watch but don't get drawn in, Solange, take big slow breaths, fine tickle of mohair between your breasts, warm waft of avocado from your own warm flesh as the girl walks ahead, Luigi's hand on her shoulder. Her hair cups her chin, falls in a straight line down her chest, swings against her breasts. Luigi's hand on her black blouse, his wide fingers knead her shoulder, but his eyes watch you, Solange. Stretch, Solange, stretch your neck your arms your long long waist, close your eyes. Their shadows, their heat, through your eyelids your skin, right in front of the couch where you sit. Luigi's hand as they drift past, hot on your shoulder, a squeeze.

Now, Solange, a slow sip, a slow smile. Later, Solange, later he will come back, look for you, silver and peach and shimmering.

Corine's voice laughing, hooting. A male voice, "Jesus Christ, Solange, come and get your dippy friend, she poured her whole goddamned drink on my frigging head." Solange opens her eyes, smiles. In the blue light by the booze table, Corine slaps her thighs, laughs and laughs. Blue, her face and lips and hair, blue in the light. A guy shakes his wet head, wipes his face with his shirt, "stupid broad's drunk. Get her away from here." Someone slaps him on the back, "Come on, you been waiting for this, you asked for it."

In the blue thick light, several guys and girls stand in a circle. Outside the circle Janice with her arms crossed over her chest. Inside the circle, Corine hoots, throws her head back, roars. Drops her head forward, her shoulders shake, retches, "Help me, Solange, help me."

Solange holds Corine's hair, Corine's blond hair through her peach fingers, the weight of Corine's sweaty head, keeps her from pitching face-first into the toilet. Corine heaves, vomits, leans her forehead against the toilet rim. "I'm dying, Solange. I'm dying, aren't I?" She lifts her face, splotchy white, bloodless lips, "Don't let me die, Solange." Drops her head over the bowl and vomits.

Corine's damp hair through her fingers, weight of Corine's head in her hand. Solange licks her lips. "You're just drunk. And pregnant."

"No, I'm dying, Solange, something's growing in me and I'm dying."

Oh, Solange, Solange, run your other hand through your smooth hair. Close your eyes. Calgary, this is Calgary. This hair, this weight in your hand, is Corine. Corine, blond and flashing eyes, marching up the Dairy Road in Bellevue, "You have to get away, Solange, you're invisible here. But you'll come back, we all do."

Corine on her knees in Calgary, not your mother naked and shivering on her hands and knees in the filthy bathroom in Bellevue. Naked and shivering. "Help me, I'm lost. Help me, I'm lost." Over and over, her voice low and moaning. Her silver-sage eyes blink when you turn on the light, stare and stare at you. "There you are. You're back. Where the hell have you been?" Her thin peach fingers around your wrist, "Don't leave me, don't ever leave me."

Wipe Corine's forehead with a cool cloth, Solange, slide your free hand into your pocket, rub your soft silk through your fingers, your soft silk name, Solange Solange.

"YOU'RE ONE OF THOSE WOMEN who grow more and more beautiful the older they get." Luigi presses his lips to her throat, probes with his tongue. Down her throat, hot then cool, to the neck of her sweater. He plays with the neckline, kisses the thin skin on her collar bones. "I had to come back. I like that other girl, but I need you." His hand strokes the mohair over her left breast, softly. "You get under my skin. Oh, Solange, please, please let me." His hand slides up under her sweater, his other hand plays with his zipper. "I'm addicted to you, Solange, I need you."

Oh, Solange, laugh softly in the dark, take both his hands in yours, guide one to your soft warm between your legs. Rub his hand up and down through your jeans. Guide the other one around your hip, to your soft round mound, your name sewn so so soft, Solange, underneath.

Wrap both legs around his buttocks, pull his hardness to you, up and down through his jeans, your jeans. "Oh God, I love you, Solange, I need you, I need to be inside you."

Up and down, his hardness, your hot soft. Oh Solange, Solange, shimmering and flowering.

Slips fully dressed off the bed where Luigi sleeps. Slips into the bathroom, stands in front of the mirror, flips on the light. Smiles at her reflection, so peach and silvery and Solange.

Slips out into the cold morning. Heads light-headed, dizzy, downhill for the river sluicing green and fishy over rocks, so many rocks.

OLIVE

Olive

"Olive? Is that you, Olive?"

"No," I say, "I'm not. My name's not Olive."

I've never seen this woman before, this woman watching me walk past the school, cross the street toward her. She paces back and forth on the curb, watching me. When I am almost across, she stops pacing, steps toward me, "Olive, is that you?"

"No," I say, looking into her eyes. Olives, I think, green olives.

"Well, you look just like her." She squints at my face. "You could be Olive."

Four pigeons flap overhead, from the house across the street where they coo up and down the steep roof, around the silver metal chimney. Coo coo coooo.

She peers into my eyes, my sunglasses hanging from a string around my neck. "Blue."

"Yes," I say, "my eyes are blue."

"Olive's eyes are blue. You could be Olive. Are you sure you're not?" Her face close to mine, staring into my eyes, hers olive green.

"Yes. I'm sure. I am not Olive." And all at once I feel caught in a lie. My black and purple pile hat, thinsulate parka, green pack bulging with apples and carrots and tofu. What if sometime between drinking my tea and brushing my teeth I was Olive? Or during the night, just before the winter sun broke the east? Or back when I was fifteen and stood out on the back porch with a paper bag in my hand and couldn't remember where I was going or why or what my name was?

"Well, you could be," she says, holding her hands in the air, big square fingers. A flowered housedress, black sweater. I hadn't noticed her flowered housedress, her calf-high rubber boots. "You could be Olive. We hung around together when we were kids."

She tucks her dress between her legs, drops her knees together, takes two steps. "You can't just pull off a pair of wet shorts you know." The corners of her mouth twitch. "Olive and me walked with our thighs together so things wouldn't fall out." She steps toward me. "Do you remember?"

"No," I say, jiggling my pack, my shins and elbows and groin suddenly remembering jumping into the pond with my friend down by the railway tracks, the friend with freckles on her nose and hands and back and chest, the friend whose body always seemed on the verge of escaping her jeans and loose shirt, "No, I don't remember."

"Hhmmm, maybe you're not Olive," she says. "Maybe you're Olive's daughter."

"No," I say, remembering the way my friend leapt into the water, arms and legs flying, remembering lying wet and *shivery on a rock in the sun, our cut-offs drying stiff and she whispered how her brother put his thing between her legs, then she sat up and laughed loud enough for everyone to hear, raced down the rock and leapt into the water, last one there's a rotten egg, and I haven't seen her for twenty years but I know she has a teenage daughter.*

From the next corner I stop to watch her stride across the street, her black sweater blowing back. Watch her stride past the school in the four-thirty winter sun, looking up and down, while another three pigeons flap overhead and a Chinook cloud wrinkles the sky.

"Good luck," I say, and wave, "good luck finding Olive."

Acknowledgements

I WOULD LIKE TO THANK everyone who read and commented on these stories. A special thanks to Lynn Podgurny, Elizabeth Haynes, Sadru Jetha, Yasmin Ladha, Andrea Davies, Cathy Ostlere, Erin Michie, Carmela Chan, Barbara Scott, Weyman Chan, Sarah Murphy and Alistair MacLeod.

My gratitude to Sandra Birdsell, as gracious and insightful an editor as you are a writer. To Coteau Books, for your hard work and dedication on behalf of writers, many thanks.

I would like to acknowledge the assistance of the Canada Council for the Arts and the Alberta Foundation for the Arts.

I am grateful as well to Lisa Hoffart, physiotherapist extraordinaire for your magical needles and healing hands.

As always, thank you Michael Whalley, my tender husband, for your friendship, support, and all the eclectic music you bring into our home.

Versions of these stories have appeared in:

"Hoar Frost": *Threshold, An Anthology of Contemporary Writing from Alberta*, edited by Srdja Pavlovic, University of Alberta Press; *Saturday Night Magazine;* CBC *Radio – The Arts Tonight*

"Tunnels": CBC *Radio – The Arts Tonight*

"Upstairs" as "Lucky Elephant": *blue buffalo magazine*

"Olive": *blue buffalo magazine*

"If a Mote": *Event Magazine*

"Hand of a Thief": *The Capilano Review, 20th Anniversary Issue*

"Long After Fathers": *Event Magazine*

"Ethel Mermaid": *blue buffalo magazine*

"Fly Away Home" as "Bellevue, Belle Vue": *Vox Magazine*

"Eleven": *Prism International.*

Ethyl Mermaid, 30 minute film, script & character direction, with director Michele Wozny, first screen-.ing at Calgary's Herland Film Festival 2003.

Photo: Jazhart Studios

About the Author

Roberta Rees' novel, *Beneath the Faceless Mountain,* set in the Crowsnest Pass, received the Alberta New Fiction Competition and the Writers Guild of Alberta Novel Award. Her poetry collection, *Eyes Like Pigeons,* won the national Gerald Lampert Award and the Writers Guild of Alberta Poetry Award. Two of her pieces have won CBC Literary Awards, in different categories. Her work has been widely published in anthologies, magazines and literary journals. A 30-minute film, *Ethyl Mermaid,* based on the story by the same name in this collection, debuted at the Herland Film Festival in Calgary.

Roberta Rees was born in New Westminster, BC, and grew up in Calgary and in the Rocky Mountains of southwestern Alberta. She currently lives and works in Calgary.

MEMBER OF SCABRINI GROUP

Québec, Canada .

2007